PRAISE FOR
KIM FU

A *TIME*, NPR, Ms. Magazine, Tor.com, Book Riot, and Shelf Awareness Best Book of the Year

"The strange and wonderful define Kim Fu's story collection, where the line between fantasy and reality fades in and out, elusive and beckoning."
—*The New York Times Book Review*

"Bold. . . . profound. . . . surreal and clever. Fu brings magical realism to exciting heights."
—*TIME*

"Memorable and utterly unique."
—*The Washington Post*

"There's something for everyone in this outstanding collection, which cements Fu as one of the most exciting short story writers in contemporary fiction."
—NPR

"Inventive and mesmerizing. . . . Vivid and surreal, readers of Carmen Maria Machado will enjoy this collection."
—BuzzFeed

"Stunning. . . . Her stories engage all the senses. . . .
A terrific collection of speculative fiction, with evocative,
textured prose that left a lasting impression."
—*Locus*

"A modern, mystical playground."
—*Thrillist*

"Will have you questioning reality and loving every minute of it."
—*Ms. Magazine*

"*Lesser Known Monsters of the 21st Century* is one
of those rare collections that never suffers from which-one-
was-that-again? syndrome. Every story here lights a flame
in the memory, shining brighter as time goes by rather than
dimming. Kim Fu writes with grace, wit, mischief, daring, and
her own deep weird phosphorescent understanding."
—**KEVIN BROCKMEIER,**
author of *The Ghost Variations*

"How I love the cool wit of these speculative stories!
Filled with wonder and wondering, they're haunted too
by loss and loneliness, their imaginative reach
profoundly rooted in the human condition."
—**PETER HO DAVIES,**
author of *A Lie Someone Told You About Yourself*

"Precise, elegant, uncanny, and mesmerizing—each story in
this collection is a crystalline gem. Kim Fu's talent is singularly
inventive, her every sentence a surprise and an adventure."
—**DANYA KUKAFKA,**
author of *Notes on an Execution*

LESSER
KNOWN
MONSTERS
OF THE
21ST
CENTURY

KIM FU

TIN HOUSE / Portland, Oregon

Published by Tin House, Portland, Oregon

Distributed by W. W. Norton & Company

Library of Congress Cataloging-in-Publication Data is available

First US Edition 2022
Printed in the USA
Interior design by Jakob Vala

www.tinhouse.com

CONTENTS

for andrea

PRE-SIMULATION CONSULTATION XF007867

—Welcome. I'll be your operator today.

—Hi.

—I see this is your first time. Why don't you start by telling me where you'd like to be, at the beginning of the simulation?

—A botanical garden. With my mother.

—Can you describe her? The way she'll be in the simulation, I mean. It doesn't necessarily have to be the way she is in real life.

—I guess—I guess I want it to be my mother right before she got sick. So she would be about sixty. Dyed-black hair, gray at the roots. She was short. Just barely five feet.

—Is your mother still alive?

—In real life?

—Yes.

—No.

—I'm sorry, but the simulation can't include deceased individuals you knew personally. It's in the handbook.

—What? Why?

—It's in the handbook.

1

—Can't you just tell me?

—It has proven to be too addictive.

—Wait—I can include dead people that I *didn't* know? Like celebrities?

—As long as they didn't specifically request to be excluded from simulations in their will. Anyone who died more than ten years ago is generally fine. Historical figures, for example. Dinner with Mozart.

—Oh, it's a lawsuit thing?

—It's more of a courtesy. We prefer to respect people's wishes.

—That sounds like a lawsuit thing.

—The requests aren't enforceable. It's functionally the same as you sitting around fantasizing about a dead celebrity—just enhanced a little bit by us. We don't broadcast or record, so it doesn't fall under life or likeness rights. You can't control someone's thoughts.

—What if I didn't tell you it was my mother? What if I said, "I'm in a botanical garden with—a woman. She's about sixty, short, dyed-black hair with white roots, looks kind of like me—"

—It wouldn't be your mother in the simulation. It would just be a short woman who looks kind of like you, in an entirely different way. The simulator hooks into your brain and its projections, and I'd need to input that it's your mother for her to appear as your mother.

—And people don't get addicted to that? To people who kind of, sort of, meet the same description?

—No.

—What if I hadn't told you she was dead? What if I'd lied and said she was alive?

—It's very important that you're honest with your operator. It's in the handbook.

—But what if I wasn't? What would happen?

—It wouldn't work.

—What does that mean?

—Best-case scenario, the simulation just wouldn't start up. Worst-case, you might experience something—glitchy.

—Like what?

—Have you ever been to a hypnotist show?

—What? Yeah, back in college.

—You know how they start out with a large group of volunteers and kick people out as they go? Until they're left with just a couple people who can be convinced that they're chickens or eating an ice cream cone or covered with ants?

—Sure.

—We have to do the opposite, here. We have to watch out for those people. We've found that the ten to fifteen percent of nonpsychotic people who are hypnotically suggestible also tend to have a looser grip on the difference between fantasy and reality. Personally, I wonder if those people have a keener appreciation of books, plays, movies, video games—if they have more immersive experiences.

—What does that—

—But the simulation, you see, requires you to have a firm grasp on what is and isn't real. We need clients to make a clean exit, such that the end of the simulation is akin to closing the book, turning off the console, walking out of the theater. It's important that you're honest with your operator, because the simulation does—interact physically with your brain.

We, the operators, also need to be absolutely certain about what is and isn't real. This is all in the handbook.

—So if I lied and said my mother was alive, and you spun it up, and we had our day at the botanical garden, what could happen?

—At the end—

—Yes?

—You might not know she died.

—Oh. Oh.

—And you'd go back to your life, expecting her to be there, and she wouldn't be. And ideally, the memory of her death and everything connected to it would come back to you on its own, once you'd talked to your friends and family, or you'd reconstruct it in such a way that it felt real enough. But it also might not. There might just be a hole there, an uncertainty that followed you for the rest of your life, that unraveled your reality around it. And that's assuming, of course, the simulation itself ran the way we scripted it.

—What do you mean? What else could happen?

—If I input the simulation on the assumption that your mother was alive, but your mind was very conscious of the fact that you lied, she could appear in both states simultaneously. Or not truly simultaneous, but flickering between them quickly enough as to appear simultaneous.

—She would appear both alive and dead.

—Yes.

—What would that even—like her corpse?

—It would depend on your conception of death. She might appear at several ages at once. She might be a ball of light, or nothing at all.

—That doesn't sound so bad.

—It can be.

—Have you seen this happen? This specific glitch?

—Yes.

—What did they see?

—It was—gruesome.

—How so?

—Their loved one had died in an accident, and they had been present. Driving. They were the driver.

—So what did they see?

—Let's get back to your session for today. Is there something else I can do for you?

—I just . . . I really only came here to see my mom.

—Perhaps you'd like to experience a particular environment? Outer space? Swimming with dolphins?

—Can I go to India?

—Absolutely! Where in India?

—I don't know. You tell me.

—Are there specific cultural sites you wish to see? Foods you want to eat?

—I . . . don't know.

—For travel experiences, I usually recommend doing some research first.

—I have to do *research*?

—Any place will be what you expect it to be. If you have a limited perception of what India is, that's what you'll experience. I can't actually send you anywhere. We just manifest your fantasies. They have to be within your capacity to fantasize.

—Well, what else do you suggest?

—Sexual fantasies have a high satisfaction rate. Also flying, always a classic. Character role play, although for that I'd recommend at least an eight-hour session, if not a full weekend—

—Hold on. You said seeing dead people you know is too addictive.

—Yes. It's in the hand—

—Sexual fantasies aren't addictive? Sex with whoever, whatever, however you want? Flying isn't addictive? What if I just said, "I want to feel perfect bliss and euphoria"? Could you do that?

—Yes.

—And that's not addictive?

—The problems with seeing deceased loved ones are well understood. For everything else, we find it's best to deal with problem clients on a case-by-case basis. Individual operators have the right to refuse any request.

—There are no other rules?

—There are de facto rules, things that no operator will do.

—Like what?

—Sex with children or real animals. Generally.

—"Real" animals? *Generally?*

—It's hard to define—

—I can fuck a dragon, but I can't see my mom?

—I'm sorry.

—There are conditions under which I can fuck a *child*, but I can't see my mom?

—No, no! Of course not! It's . . . There's a degree of discernment in . . . We live in a society in which anything intimate or unusual is treated as sexual, and that sometimes . . . If a client asks to be held in the palm of a giant, is that sexual?

—I mean, probably.

—So if they asked to be held in the palm of a giant child, you would refuse, if you were an operator?

—I suppose.

—You can't imagine a way in which being held by a giant child could be fun? Whimsical? In a nonsexual way?

—I guess it would depend on, I don't know, where they were going with it? How they said it?

—See, that's exactly—

—Can I murder someone?

—That . . . depends.

—Are you kidding me? I can murder someone, but I can't—

—If someone comes in here and wants to rehearse stalking and strangling his ex-wife or shooting up his office, the operator is going to say no. But if he wants to, I don't know, be a gunslinger in an old western—

—Ah, so I can be an action hero?

—We can do that.

—Mow down bad guys, save the damsel?

—Is that what you'd like?

—Do I have to tell you what I want the bad guys to look like?

—Ideally, yes. In broad strokes at least.

—What if I want them all to be a specific race?

—I . . .

—Well?

—I would say no to that.

—And if I didn't specify? If I said that I didn't care what they look like? What would happen?

—I'd sketch something in, but the simulation would be influenced by what your perception of a "bad guy" is.

—So if my perception of a "bad guy" just happens to be—

—I see where you're going with this.

—And *you* would say no. But if I had a different operator, if one of my Klan buddies worked here—

—Nobody here would—

—Or just an operator with a different philosophy on the whole thing. "Oh, they're just blowing off steam. It's all in good fun. It's not real."

—The simulation is just a platform. It's a machine, a venue. Your brain creates the majority of the content. We can't dictate every—

—But there is one hard no. Violent racist fantasies, a naked hot tub party with Einstein and a unicorn, that's fine. That's up to the discretion of the operator. But I can't look at some flowers with my mom. I can't talk to her one last time.

[silence]

—Shall we see about getting you a refund?

—The handbook said there are no refunds under any circumstances.

—You read the handbook.

—The refund policy is on the cover.

—Most people have a very positive experience.

—Having sex with unicorns.

—You're really hung up on the unicorn thing.

—Well, what else do people do? What's the best fantasy someone came in here with? That made them the happiest?

—There's a section in the handbook on how to make the most of your—

—The best one you've seen, personally, as operator.

—Me?

—Yes.

—No one's ever asked me that before. [silence] It was a musical.

—A musical?

—In the simulation, he was the writer, composer, and director of a Broadway musical. I suggested that he choose a specific musical, and we'd make it so that in the simulation, it would be as if he wrote it. He insisted that it had to be an original show. I explained that everything in it, then, would be vague. Just the feeling and suggestion of music and dance, blurred and nonspecific, cobbled together out of other things he'd seen and heard—much like India would have been for you. But it turned out I'd misunderstood him. He'd actually written a musical, in the real world. Sort of. He'd been working on it most of his life. He had the main melodies and lyrics. He could see the choreography and costumes in his mind.

—Was it any good?

—Of course not. It was terrible. But we put together a hell of a show.

—I don't understand.

—In the simulation, it wasn't what it was, but what he dreamed it could be.

—Are you okay?

—That was a good day. That was a day that made me feel good about being an operator. [silence] It is a lawsuit thing.

—What?

—The reason you can't see your mom. The simulator is inherently addictive. Everything people do here is addictive. A small number of our clients make up the majority of our

9

business. The "whales," rich people who come as much as they can afford, and then some. People who come every day until they're bankrupt. But the ones addicted to superpowers or sex or the simulator itself don't win in civil court. Nobody pities them. Everyone says, "Oh, the simulation is just a platform. They ruined their lives themselves with how they chose to use it." But if we—if we advertise that someone can see their dead child again, they can see their village before the war, they can have a version of their life where their family is intact, go back to before it was shattered, they can live just one ordinary day without grief . . . And if they choose to live inside that fantasy, if they choose to forsake the real world and all its sorrows—then we're the bad guys. We're exploiting the bereaved. It also just . . . happened so much. Especially around certain disasters. And it wasn't . . . Operators would quit.

[silence]

—Did the musical guy come back?

—No. Not that I know of. He just wanted to see it once.

—What if I promise never to come back?

—I can't. I'm sorry. I'll get fired.

—Is it hard-coded in? The rule?

—No. We're just not supposed to.

—But you said the simulations aren't recorded or broadcast. They're supposed to be one hundred percent confidential. That was also on the cover. How would anyone know?

—When you come back. When you keep coming back.

—What if I just tell you about it, what I want? And then you decide?

—I'm telling you, I can't.

—It's nothing. It's really nothing. It's boring, it's easy. It's so small, what I want. [silence] Okay. So my mom and I are at the botanical garden, inside the conservatory—

—What does it look like?

—The conservatory?

—Yes, where you are. You have to describe it for me. All the details that matter to you.

—It has a domed glass roof, made of triangular sections.

—What time of day?

—Early afternoon, middle of the day. A weekday. I took it off from work. Blue sky.

—How big is the building? Can you see the whole thing from where you're standing?

—No.

—What plants are immediately around you?

—We're in the tropical rainforest section. Pink bromeliads, dwarf palms, a banana tree. Butterflies.

—What else is important?

—We're walking through the gardens together. She's holding my arm. She's telling me plant facts, boring ones, like "Did you know bamboo can grow a full inch in just an hour?" And she's gossiping about relatives I don't remember, and kids I went to elementary school with. "Little Russell is a news-caster now! Aunt Sandy is pregnant!" That sort of thing. And I'm just listening. I say things like, "That's interesting," and "Russell did love to hear himself talk." I'm not getting snide or impatient, or looking at my phone, or thinking about work, or picking a fight.

—And then?

—Nothing. That's it. We do that until my time is up. [silence] Are you surprised it's not something more dramatic?

—No. I told you, it's often—ordinary things.

—So what do you think?

—The simulations aren't recorded, but these conversations are.

—What?

—Pre-simulation consultations are recorded as a text transcript.

—I thought everything was confidential.

—The transcripts are anonymized, and they're not reviewed by a human being, just an AI. And it tends to be—somewhat literal-minded. It's not very good at telling when people are lying or being sarcastic, and the transcripts obviously don't contain our expressions or gestures. Do you understand?

—I—

—So, no, I can't do that. I can't simulate a walk in the conservatory with your mother. Under the distant domed roof, triangles of blue sky, palm leaves overhanging your path. Your mother delighted when a butterfly lands on her shoulder. And you, patient and kind and present as you wish you had been, just once. I would get fired. Tell me something else you want.

—The only thing I—

—Just tell me something else.

—I want to . . . ride a unicorn.

—Great. I'll start the input and mapping process. Please head next door, where you'll be fitted for the simulator cap. Usually, if I have any questions, I'll use the room-to-room communicator, but this time I expect I—won't have any.

—Will you—see what I see?

—Yes.

—Will I see you again?

—No. If you keep your promise.

—Then, thank you. Thank you.

—Enjoy your unicorn.

—I will.

LIDDY, FIRST TO FLY

Liddy showed us her ankles during first recess. She lifted the cuffs of her blue corduroys, first one and then the other, as we sat by the broken picnic table in the patch of grass between the parking lot and the basketball court. Chloe and Liddy sat on the table, their feet on what remained of the bench. Mags and I sat in the grass, avoiding the jagged wood. Raised white bumps protruded from Liddy's skin, one on the outside of each ankle, each a few inches above the rounded knob of bone—perfectly symmetrical.

"Blisters from your boots?" I said.

"I don't think so."

Chloe tapped on her phone. "Ringworm," she said, holding out her screen.

Mags recoiled. "Oh, gross. Oh my God."

Liddy stopped poking at the bumps just long enough to glance over. "It doesn't look like that."

"Maybe you should go to the doctor," I said.

"They just look like zits to me," Mags said. "Big ones."

"My mom won't take me to the doctor for some zits on my legs."

"Can you stop being gross and showing them to us, then?" Chloe said, still fiddling with her phone. "We've wasted almost the whole recess."

Simon L. ran by, chasing an escaped basketball. "Dogs pee there!" he shouted at me and Mags. "You're sitting in dog pee!"

Liddy showed us her ankles again the next day. Only Chloe sat on the table, the remaining three of us in the grass. Liddy laid her legs across my lap, and I lifted her sneaker close to my face. The bumps had grown, the skin noticeably thinning as it stretched, becoming translucent. "There's something in there," she said.

Something did appear to be pushing up through Liddy's skin, the size and shape of the tip of a pen, only white. "Maybe Chloe was right, and you do have worms," I said.

"Ringworm is caused by a fungus," Chloe corrected.

I couldn't resist poking at it. "It's hard, though. Would a worm be hard?"

Mags was looking over my shoulder, transfixed. "Ew. Ew, ew, ew."

"Does it hurt?" I asked.

"It's more . . . uncomfortable. Like I can feel how tight the skin is. Like wearing clothes that are too small."

"It looks like bone," Chloe declared, from above.

"It's weird that they're in the exact same place," I said. "It's almost like someone ran something straight through both of your ankles. Like the bolts on the neck of the monster in

16

Frankenstein. Or Mags's dog when he broke his leg and got that plate put on it."

"Did you break your ankles and not remember?" Mags said.

We let this pass, as a Mags thing to say. "Anyway, you should go to the doctor," I concluded.

"I don't want to bug my mom with this," Liddy said, pulling her pant legs back down. "She's got a lot going on right now."

Mags let out a horrified squeal.

"Wow," I said.

"Shit," Chloe said.

Liddy stood in front of us, holding up the cuffs of her jeans. The bumps were now bubbles of clear fluid, about the diameter of a quarter, the skin almost completely transparent. Within each one was a coil of something dark and unrecognizable, bringing to mind matted hair, a clog pulled up from a drain.

"You should go to the hospital," I said. Mags nodded.

Chloe typed swiftly on her phone. "Maybe Mags was right, and they're just blackheads. Sometimes people get huge ones that look kind of like that. See?"

Liddy looked at Chloe's phone. "So should I pop them?"

"Is it weird that I *want* you to pop them?" Mags said. "Like, I really, really want you to."

"Me too," I said. Looking at them was almost painful, like watching an oblong, overfilled water balloon bounce across the scraped concrete of a pool deck.

"This website says you should sterilize a needle to do it, to prevent infection."

"Can we watch?" Mags asked.

Chloe looked up from her phone with a disgusted expression. "Mags!"

"Sure," Liddy said. "You and Grace can come over after school. My mom won't be home until late. She has a date."

"I'm coming too!" Chloe insisted.

While Liddy hosed off her legs in the shower, Chloe lit a candle in Liddy's bedroom—a scented leftover from Christmas, filling the room with the waxy, candy-sweet smell of artificial pine needles. She ran a sewing needle through the flame. Once it was cool, she dipped it in rubbing alcohol and left it to dry on a paper towel. Liddy sat on her bed, her feet up on a clean white towel taken from the hall closet. We were going for a surgical atmosphere, or a ceremonial one—an appendectomy, a baptism—but instead it felt more like a game of pretend, the kind of game we'd only recently outgrown.

Chloe and I sat on Liddy's bed with her. Mags sat on the floor, resting her elbows on the mattress with her chin in her hands, her face level with the bulbous horrors.

Liddy pressed the needle to her skin lengthwise, parallel to her leg, and slid it down to pierce the first of the two bubbles. We instinctively all leaned away, as though it would explode, but Liddy had to draw the needle up to tear through the outside layer of skin. Clear fluid ran down her leg. She mopped it up with a hand towel.

When she lifted the towel away, we could see the matted clump that had been underneath, resembling a downy, slimy, just-birthed animal, newly ejected from its mother. Liddy got up and went back to the bathroom, and we followed. She left the shower curtain open as she stood in the tub and splashed the lump with tap water.

The coil unfurled. She turned off the water and fluffed it out with another towel, helping it along. "They're . . . feathers," I said.

A bird's wing stuck straight out from the side of her leg, the feathers black, the span approximately the length of her hand. The wing flexed away from Liddy, stretching to its full outward distance, before trembling and folding back, the tip pointing down once more.

One by one, we called our mothers and asked if we could stay the night at Liddy's. One by one, our mothers said no, but we could stay for dinner. My mother asked if she could talk to Liddy's, and I lied that she was in the bathroom and couldn't come to the phone. Dinner was a vague concept; we could reasonably stay until bedtime before Chloe's parents would call her phone and the rest of our parents would call Liddy's house phone.

Liddy lanced the remaining bubble, freeing the other wing. Clean and dry, folded down in a relaxed position against the sides of her legs, they were beautiful, with an oily, iridescent blue sheen, like crows' necks in a certain light. They looked ornamental, an intentional contrast to her milky skin and the downy blond hair on her legs, like part of a circus performer's costume.

The things we said, at first, just reasserted the obvious: Are those really growing out of your legs, are those really wings? And then details: Does it hurt? (Not really.) Can you control them? (Liddy focused, experimentally, and the tips of the wings would drift a fraction of an inch; she couldn't get them to unfurl completely again, and she couldn't control them individually—"Like you can't flare just one of your nostrils," she explained.)

"Why aren't they growing out of your back?" Chloe asked. "Like an angel? It would be sexier if they grew out of your back." Chloe was always making strange, knowing declarations of this kind.

"Do you think you can fly?" Mags asked.

"They feel . . . stuck," Liddy said, again making the wings ruffle faintly. "Like they want to open and lift again, but there's something in the way."

"You should probably tell your mom now," I said.

"Yeah, I should," Liddy said, looking down at her softly twitching wings, with a faraway expression that meant she wouldn't.

There was a way in which Liddy's wings didn't strike us as extraordinary. The realm of pretend had only just closed its doors to us, and light still leaked through around the edges. Everything was baffling and secretive then, especially our own bodies, sprouting all kinds of outgrowths that were meant to be hidden, desperately ignored and not discussed, hairs and lumps that could be weaponized against us. On some level, it seemed like this would just be part of Liddy's eventual adulthood, tucking her wings beneath sensible slacks and off to the office, just as our mothers scooped and flattened and plucked themselves raw.

And though we never would have admitted it, we were growing bored of each other. We couldn't actually remember how or why we became friends. It was a story our mothers told: what we said when we came home from our first day of kindergarten, inexplicably enamored with each other, a story that embarrassed us now.

I wasn't in the same class as the other three anymore. I had a classroom friend; we talked only during class and went our separate ways during lunch and recess. And sometimes—often—I realized I'd rather be talking to her about our egg launcher for science class, or the books we were reading, and that all I felt for Chloe, Mags, and Liddy was a kind of loyalty-bond, an obligation. Mags had joined the children's choir at her church, sometimes Liddy's mom gave her money to go to drop-in intramural dodgeball at the community center, and Chloe was spending as much time with a glamorous older cousin as the cousin would allow. They would talk about these other friends in a way that made me aware of us drifting.

Now we had something to bond us again, a new hidden world.

Liddy didn't come to school for three days. We assumed that I'd been wrong about that look on her face, that Liddy showed her mother and the adult, bureaucratic machine kicked in. We'd see Liddy on the cover of *Scientific American* or *Weekly World News*, or she was in the hospital, getting her wings surgically removed. We imagined a tall, menacing doctor leaning over her as she drifted under anesthesia, saying, "Don't worry, you'll be a normal girl again soon," and digging the bones of her wings out from under her skin, those lovely, shining feathers tearing away in a mass of blood and viscera. (Chloe was the chief architect of these nightmares.)

On the fourth day, I called Liddy's house in the morning, after breakfast. Her mother picked up, and I asked how Liddy was doing, said we missed her at school. "Oh, how sweet of you to worry, Grace," she said. "Liddy is fine. She just left for school, in fact. She had what my mother used to call a 'growing fever.' Do you get those?"

"No? I don't think so. I don't know what that is."

"I had them at your age. A fever that lasts a few days, you sleep the whole time, and you wake up a teeny bit taller. Part of the growing spurts you're all going through."

"Oh. Uh, I'm glad Liddy is feeling better." I hesitated. "And nothing else was wrong with her?"

"That's the funny thing about growing fevers! How you know it's not the flu or something else. You don't have any other symptoms. You just sleep it off."

Liddy's mom always sounded excessively cheerful, and it made me uncomfortable, like she was constantly lying. I wanted to ask if she had also sprouted wings at our age. I tried to remember if I'd ever seen her bare legs, if she'd ever joined us in the public pool in the summertime. Would Liddy ever be able to go to the pool again? "I better get to school," I said, finally.

When I arrived at school, I saw Liddy for just a moment across the blacktop before the first bell rang and everyone went inside. I couldn't catch up to her in time to talk, but from that distance, she did look taller somehow, her cheeks a little more refined, her blond hair a little darker than before.

Liddy didn't come out at first recess. Mags, who was in her class, reported that she'd stayed behind to talk to the teacher about what she'd missed while she was out sick. At lunch, we clustered behind the lone tree near the picnic table. We were visible from the parking lot but not from the basketball court. Liddy was wearing navy blue sweatpants, loose legs with an elastic cuff at the bottom. When she pulled them up, the cuffs held just below her knee.

The wings had grown dramatically. The point where each one connected to her leg had expanded up and down—no longer a point but a line, a full joint, stretching from just above her ankle to just below her knee. Folded down, against her leg, each wing traced the same curve as her calf muscle, rounded at the top, tapered toward the ground.

"I've been practicing," Liddy said. She glanced around, making sure no one could see us, and then stood with her feet apart, her legs forming an inverted V. The wings spread to a majestic span, flexing concave and convex as she flapped them slowly, back to front. They were angled slightly down and behind her, and their curving shape made the lowest, outermost part of each wing drag in the loose dirt, throwing up small, smokelike trails of dust. When Liddy stilled the wings and folded them down again, they were noticeably stained by the lighter-colored earth.

We were too stunned to speak at first, but I found I was quickly thinking about the mechanics. I'd had science right before lunch, where I'd been working on my egg launcher with my class friend. It wouldn't just be sexier, as Chloe had said, for Liddy's wings to be embedded between her shoulder blades, but more useful, too. She couldn't get any lift with her wings scraping along the ground that way, and it intuitively seemed like it would take more force to get off the ground, with most of her weight *above* the wings, than if they'd appeared somewhere higher up on her body. They also seemed proportionally small, if one pictured Liddy as a bird, especially with her heavy, human skeleton, rather than hollow bird bones.

I started to explain some of this—why I didn't think Liddy would be able to fly. Chloe interrupted, "We don't know what Liddy's bones are like. She's pretty light. Maybe the wings aren't the only thing that's different about her."

"They do drag on the ground, though," Mags said.

"Maybe if you jump?" Chloe suggested.

"Maybe Liddy is like an ostrich or a dinosaur," I said. "They're not for flying, but they'd help stabilize her when she runs."

"Or she's like a chicken," Mags supplied. "She can fly, just not much."

"I think I can fly," Liddy said. Her voice, I thought, had a new authority to it, was even slightly deeper than before. It broke us out of our speculative reverie, out of pretend. "I just haven't figured out how, yet."

"Try jumping," Chloe said. Liddy jumped straight up in the air twice; each time, there was only a half second of suspension, in which the wings fluttered frantically, not the full, swooping gesture she'd shown us before. "You need to jump from higher up," Chloe said.

A basketball bounced past us, and Simon L. came running after it. Liddy tugged down the legs of her sweatpants a little too aggressively, and the low waist came down, showing the top inch of her pink underwear.

"The girls are showing each other their underwear!" Simon crowed, returning to the court. "They're back there pulling their pants down!"

We stood close together, eyeing Simon with disdain. We'd been told we would develop a new interest in boys. They would suddenly become intriguing, infuriating, and looking at them would make us sweat our new, ranker sweat. For me that had not happened. Boys seemed yet more distant, less interesting, as the girls around me morphed in ways that were truly fascinating. As they grew wings.

After school, we went to Mags's house. Their family had a large, hilly, fenced-in backyard. At the back of the lot was a grassy plateau atop a twelve-foot retaining wall, the rear of the house opening onto a smaller rise, a bowl-shaped valley between them. In the winter, the long slope below the wall was perfect for sledding.

From the ledge of the stone wall, the drop seemed higher than we expected, the grass below not quite as lush, a bare patch here and there. Liddy stood at the edge, her wings spread and puffed out, her back to us. She faced the sun in the western sky, the light haloed around her.

Liddy took a small, neat jump forward, her feet leaving the ground at the same time. Her wings flapped fully just once, forward and back, before she hit the ground. She landed on her feet but tripped almost immediately, tumbling, somersaulting down the curving lawn. When she recovered onto her side, she was at the lowest part of the bowl.

"Liddy?" Mags called. "Are you okay?"

Liddy jumped to her feet so quickly it startled us. She came running up the hill, scrambling back onto the ledge with us before we knew it. "I feel like I had something there," she said, panting. Her gray T-shirt had fresh grass stains, and dirt was embedded in the skin of her forearms.

"We should do an experiment," I suggested. "One of us should jump off at the same time as you. Then we could see if your wings actually slow your fall or give you any lift."

"I'll do it," Chloe said. She stood from where she'd been sitting with her legs dangling off the ledge, brushing off the seat of her pants. Her expression, incredibly, seemed bored, in need of a change, in need of attention.

Liddy was still catching her breath. "I want to do a running jump this time. See if I can get more air."

"You guys have to try and jump at the exact same time in the exact same way," I said.

"Sure, whatever," Chloe said.

Liddy peered over the edge, and then took a few steps backward. "Let's start from here," she said, directing Chloe to stand beside her. "Mags, say, 'One-two-three, go!'"

"One-two-three, go!"

They ran to the edge. At the last second, her feet already in space, Chloe seemed to change her mind, awkwardly fumbling in midair as she fell with a shriek. Liddy released one foot and then the other with intention, arcing outward as she jumped, looking graceful and fearless. Her black feathers glistened and her wings audibly sliced through the air, a whooshing rush. All the same, she landed only a moment later than Chloe, if at all. Chloe landed in a crouch, and then sat back on her butt in the same spot. Liddy rolled all the way down the rest of the hill again. And again, she popped right up, hurtling toward us. It was unnerving, like a zombie in a movie who's been hit by a baseball bat but won't stay down. Chloe took her time, groaning as she pulled herself to her feet, trailing behind.

"That was better than the first time," Liddy said, hoisting herself onto the ledge. "I really think I've almost got it." There was dirt in her hair and streaked across the side of her cheek.

Chloe came up after her. "Je-ee-sus, that was scary," she said. "I am *not* doing that again."

Just then, Mags's mom stepped out through the sliding glass back door and into the yard. She called out to us. "Mags?"

"Hi, Mom," Mags called back. Liddy's wings were folded flat, unlikely to be visible at this distance.

"I just got home. What are you girls doing up there?"

"Just, you know, playing."

"Well, be careful not to fall!" she said. Chloe giggled behind her hand. "Do you girls want a snack?"

"We're fine, Mom."

"Have you seen your brother?"

"He's in his room."

"Your brother is *home?*" Chloe hissed. "What the hell! What if he'd looked out his window?"

"He's in there playing games on his computer. He never comes out or raises his blinds," Mags said. "I kind of forget he exists."

Mags's mom called out to us again. "It's going to get dark soon. Maybe your friends should start getting ready to go home, and you should get started on your homework?"

"Sure thing, Mom."

As soon as the sliding door clicked shut, Liddy announced, "Okay, I'm going to jump again."

"You can't. My mom might see."

Liddy let out an exasperated noise through her nose, like a horse. "This isn't high enough, anyway. I don't have enough time in the air."

"Any higher wouldn't be safe," I said.

"I'm pretty sure we could've killed ourselves just from this height if we'd fallen the wrong way," Chloe said. Liddy paced back and forth along the ledge. "You know where you should try?" Chloe went on. "The Springboard."

My mom had pointed out the Springboard to me when we drove past, clucking her tongue in disapproval. It was a place along the shore where a high cliffside jutted out over the ocean, where teenagers went to jump and dive in the summer. The tip of the rock outcropping was vaguely squared off, like a diving board. Officially, it'd been cordoned off for the last five years with a stout fence and a sign with red-on-white lettering, but that hadn't stopped anyone. Every summer, some kid broke their leg or arm, and the columnist in our local paper called for a higher fence. And over the decades, six teenagers had died, oddly in clusters: four one summer in the 1970s, and two the year they put up the fence. My mom was friends with the mother of the kid who'd died most recently.

That Saturday, in the late morning, we told our parents we were going to the mall and walked the two miles along the two-lane highway to get to the Springboard. It was too early in the year and in the day for anyone else to be there, but in the daylight, there was a risk that we would be spotted from the road. We'd dressed in dark colors to better blend into the narrow band of spruce trees that separated the roadway from the cliffs.

We hopped the fence with ease. Liddy peered over the edge. Mags asked, "How do people get hurt doing this?"

"Mostly they fall off the wrong part of the cliff while waiting for their turn," I said, "where the water is sometimes too shallow, in low tide. They're usually drunk or high, and there's a lot of them, and someone just gets crowded off."

"So nobody gets hurt if they go off the actual Springboard?"

"No, sometimes people just hit the water wrong, or the tide is strong and they get scraped up while they're swimming back."

"What about the kids who died?" Liddy asked. I watched her take off her hoodie and her T-shirt before answering. Underneath, she had on a black one-piece bathing suit that I'd never seen. Last summer, we'd all gotten matching tankinis—mine had been turquoise with stripes, and Liddy's had been rose pink with darker pink flowers. Her new suit was plain, the neckline a simple, austere scoop in the front and the back, the armpits cut deep.

I'd looked up the news articles, but they didn't say. Chloe looked them up right then on her phone and couldn't find anything more. Everything I knew came from my mom, and I didn't know where her information came from. "They always question if it could have been suicide," I said. "Especially the last kid who died that summer in the seventies—he was the boyfriend of one of the girls who died, and he was alone when it happened."

"That's weirdly romantic," Mags said.

"Rita's done it dozens of times," Chloe piped up, referring to her older cousin. "And she doesn't have wings."

Over her swimsuit, Liddy was still wearing the sweatpants she'd worn all week. The ocean was loud where we were, carefully toward the center of the outcropping, away from the edges. We sat in silence for a few moments. A seagull cried out in the distance.

"Are you scared?" Mags asked.

After a beat, Liddy replied, "No. It's weird. It's like there's a part of my brain that knows I should be, but I just don't feel it."

When Liddy stood and added her sweatpants to the stack of her clothes, I had the sudden sense that we were saying goodbye. The spandex sheen of her black bathing suit matched the sheen on her feathers. I imagined the feathers growing up her legs, spreading, merging with her suit. I saw her blunt-cut blond hair darkening, wrapping around the sides of her head, puffing out as yet more feathers. I imagined this strange, upside-down bird creature with my old friend's blue eyes, and I saw it leap, saw the first powerful thrust of its wings as it lifted off. I saw it fly straight into the sun, vanish over the horizon. And I felt sad, but happy for her too. She had become what she was meant to be, and maybe we all would.

As in Mags's yard, Liddy took a few steps back to take a running start. Just as she started to sprint for the end of the board, we heard rustling in the woods we'd just come through.

It was our mothers, pushing through the trees as a unit, with Mags's mom leading the pack. "There they are!" she shouted. "Girls! What in God's name are you doing here?"

Liddy's mom screamed.

Liddy had disappeared over the edge. Mags and Chloe were both on their hands and knees, crawling to the end to peer down at where Liddy had jumped. And I knew, suddenly, without looking, what they saw, what the mothers pushing past me would see as well: a girl with long, pale, unremarkable legs, falling fast, straight down into the ocean like a rock.

I knew because all of the mothers were here. If it had been one adult, the magic could have lasted. One adult can be lured into pretend, can taste the tea in our toy cup, hear the voice on the toy phone. One adult could have seen what we saw and carried it quietly within her forever. But not four. Four adults have to agree on what happened, agree on the rules. Four adults can talk to each other until reality straightens, until doubt is crushed, until their memories unstitch and reform. Four adults never see a miracle at once. Liddy's wings would dissolve into the air or reabsorb into her skin without leaving a mark.

I still hoped Liddy would swoop up, flying past us, laughing with joy. But now Liddy's mother was running in the other direction, scrambling and jumping down the stomped-down path to the beach where the cliff divers eventually swam up. My mother and Chloe's followed, while Mags's mother stayed with us on the cliff, shouting at us and staring worriedly down below.

You might ask: Where were our fathers? Why was it only our mothers who were pulled from their Saturday routines for this—Liddy's from work and the rest from home, from leisure, from caring for our siblings? And which one of us told, left the telltale clue? All of us would deny it later.

The three of us watched from above as Liddy's mom ran straight out into the ocean, fully dressed in her dental hygienist scrubs. We were all kneeling, more aware of the height than before. The sun made the water a blazing silver, dizzying to look at.

And then we saw Liddy's head pop up out of the water. Her hair did look darker than before, more amber brown than her true blond, but I suppose that's because it was wet. She swam cleanly toward her mother. She paused to tread a few feet away. Her mother was up to her chest in the water, and we could tell she was still screaming, though not what she was saying. Liddy eventually, reluctantly, dog-paddled a little closer, her feet still not touching the sand below, and her mother grabbed her by the arm. As her mother jerked her forward, Liddy's head dunked under.

I ran for the beach. Mags's mother went to stop me but I dodged around her, jumping and running down the rocks and crushed beach grass. When I got there, Liddy and her mother were out of the water. Liddy was on her hands and knees, her head hanging down, her sopping-wet hair draped over her face. Her mother stood before her, fuming and raving, her scrubs soaked to the skin. She didn't seem to notice what I, and my mother, and Chloe's mother, were all staring at: the drenched, salt-ruined mass of feathers clinging to both of Liddy's legs.

TIME CUBES

The Time Cubes kiosk appeared in the main hall about a month before Christmas. Alice joined the crowd gathered around the vendor demonstrating the toys. Sandwiched between his open palms, he held a clear acrylic box, about a foot tall, a foot wide, and a foot deep, with a knob on one side that resembled an old-fashioned dimmer switch. The box contained a spindly green plant with heart-shaped leaves, planted in a glass jar. Behind him, on the shelves of the kiosk, lay a dozen identical boxes.

The salesman slowly spun the knob on the box in his hands, turning it toward himself. The leaves, previously still, at first undulated in an unseen wind. Then they began to shrink. At their smallest, they gathered at the stem and folded together like the pages of a book, curled back into buds. The central stalk receded until the entire plant had vanished into the soil.

He reversed course, turning the knob the other way. Within the box, the show proceeded in the proper order: a fresh shoot appearing in the jar of dirt, the plant growing and sprouting.

Until—unnervingly—he turned the knob past its original starting point. The plant expanded until it overgrew its container. Tendrils curved and wrapped where they hit the walls, and leaves pushed up against the transparent plastic like faces, fogging up the surface. The plant reached a glorious, full-crested peak, a jungle of one.

Then, choked, the leaves began to wilt and droop, shriveling to ribbons. The stalk tilted unsteadily in one direction, hunched over as though humbled. Eventually, bare brown wires hung over the edges of the jar like stringy human hair.

Alice clapped along with a few others, an uncertain smattering of applause that disappeared in the high ceilings of the main hall that smothered all sound. The toy seller turned the knob back and forth casually now, resurrecting and killing the plant, making it bigger and smaller, whipping it between full-grown and a seedling, a mere idea in the dark earth. As the knob spun rapidly, another effect became more noticeable: the box was lit up inside, by no obvious fixture—no visible bulbs or wiring—and the light flickered and strobed almost imperceptibly, similar to Alice's vision when she was so exhausted that her eyelids twitched.

"Who wants to buy?"

The adults hesitated, a few children started to beg. The price was high, on par with a new, high-end smartphone. A lot to pay for an educational life-cycle toy that would likely end up forgotten in a toy chest by New Year's. But they itched to take a Time Cube apart, to smash it open and see how it worked. If it was a holograph, it was better than any holographic technology Alice had ever seen, better than the porn, the billboards, the concerts, the holo-phones that had appeared in commercials as prototypes in development but had yet to materialize in stores. The plant looked real and substantial from every angle, and there was nowhere in the borderless box to hide a projector. Without the gaudy, backlit sign—*Time Cubes!*—one would assume the kiosk sold terrariums.

"Okay," the toy seller said. "I see you're not convinced." From below the counter, he pulled out another clear plastic cube. "This is the slightly more expensive model," he said.

At first, it was hard to see what was inside. It seemed like just more plants, a couple of hand-sized ferns, a thin layer of muddy water at the bottom with a branch laid across. Eventually, Alice registered movement—the pulsing under-chin of a bulbous, nearly spherical frog, black leopard spots across his green back.

The vendor wiggled his fingers and eyebrows, stuck the tip of his tongue out in pantomime of concentration. None of the children laughed.

He turned the knob backward. The frog began to twitch and wander through the cramped space, always reversing, his back legs stepping before the front, pausing at intervals. The back end of the frog winnowed into a tail as he slimmed down, as his dark, opaque flesh lightened to brown lace. At the point where he resembled a four-legged fish, he leapt onto the wall of the box facing the audience. Affixed there, he shrank to a black blotch, the distinctive ink-drop of a tadpole, which then slid down the wall until it came to rest in the puddle at the bottom, a black spot in a gooey bubble, and here the knob clicked as it hit its end—that was as far as it could turn. They would not see the frog's parents materialize out of the air.

As the vendor turned the knob in the other direction, he sped through the stages they had just seen, as though bored. Egg to tadpole to froglet to frog, fascinating but familiar from any number of nature shows. When the adult frog was back in his sedentary position on the branch, Alice saw a woman near the front cover her mouth with one hand, and someone else started applauding again, a little frantically, trying to stop the demonstration here. Alice and the rest of the crowd did not join in, did not clap. They leaned in, pitching forward and rising up, shoulders expanding away from their waists, taking a deep, collective breath.

The frog didn't age in any obvious way, and he moved less in adulthood, his stillness making the flickering of the light more apparent. Abruptly, in one motion, his legs splayed out underneath him, as though he were crushed by an invisible fist from above. A frenzy of movement followed, a staticky shadow cast over the frog and the murky puddle surrounding him, replacing his eyes with empty holes, deflating the body while leaving the skin relatively intact: a frog-skin rug, a silhouette. At last, the shadow dispersed, and the wild, crimped angles of the frog's skeleton were all that remained. The knob clicked with an air of finality.

One little boy, his eyes crushed to slits between his high cheeks and low forehead, said flatly, seemingly to no one in particular, "You have to buy me that. You *have* to."

Alice's Depressive Specialist said they were living in a paradise, and Alice had to agree, in the sense that the recent past was worse, the future would almost certainly be worse, and the present was worse for most other people, living elsewhere. She said that Alice's thoughts and fears were extremely common, as Depressives were now a plurality, exceeding any other categorization. She said this like it was supposed to be comforting.

Alice identified as a Depressive Insider, the latter designation meaning she did not leave the Mall. She lived on the seventy-fifth floor of the south tower and she worked as a lab tech on basement five of the east tower; her Depressive Specialist was two floors up on east basement two. Alice didn't even go out onto the skybridges that connected the four towers anymore, preferring the tunnels and indoor connectors. The skybridges were always extremely crowded, for one thing, everyone pressed to the gaps in the open fencing, staring at the dim red medallion of sun or moon. In the winter, the air was hot and damp, and the rest of the year, an irritating dust blew through, tearing into your eyes and throat—sometimes a color like powdered rust that stained your clothes, sometimes a reeking sulfurous yellow, sometimes sparkling and colorless like crushed diamonds.

The fencing prevented jumpers, so there was really no appeal for Alice.

Alice's Depressive Specialist suggested she try dating or casual sex as a way to lift her mood. She recommended location-based apps; proximity would limit the energy and motivation required, and if she turned on the path-matching feature, she would likely be matched with other Insiders. "But base your search primarily on physical attractiveness," she said. "Just go for someone sexy."

Like most other things on her phone, the dating apps were lulling and hypnotic. When she played with them, she forgot what she was supposed to be doing, what the goal was, comforted by the light of the screen and the swiping gestures, the same ones that had soothed her as an infant. She tried to look at people passing her in the Mall corridors, the people crammed in with her in the elevator, but their faces came apart the longer she stared at them. Their features clustered in new ways, piles of eyeballs and noses and mouths that she didn't know how to judge as sexy/not-sexy.

Through December, when Alice wasn't working or with her Depressive Specialist, she usually found herself back at the Time Cube kiosk, watching the seller's demonstration. The plant and the frog, alive and then dead and then alive. To her surprise, it didn't seem like they sold well, despite the large crowd stopping up the flow of pedestrian traffic in the main hall. She would have bought one if she could have afforded it.

The vendor was about her age, maybe slightly younger. He looked like someone who cared for his appearance tenderly, with small, vain touches, like grace notes on a sheet of music. His clothes were neatly pressed, his shoes shined, his skin uncommonly even and smooth—porcelain with a rosy glow under the eyes, bringing to mind a Renaissance portrait. And because she spent so much time watching him, his face and hands, with their magician flourishes and waggles, developed a comforting familiarity, like the faces of her lab mates and her dead parents in dreams. She could round all of this up to "sexy."

On her day off, after the vendor pulled the rollaway walls down over his kiosk and locked it up at the end of the day, she followed him to the dining hall. He went to the one on the fourth floor of the west tower that Alice rarely visited. She preferred basement six north, where the food stalls were identical, save the signs indicating the shapes and flavors of the patties: steel countertops between evenly spaced white laminate pillars, hundreds of identical seats at identical tables in a grid pattern in the center, the lighting soft but bright—sterile and undemanding, like her lab. West four, instead, traded in nostalgia. The "taco" stand served out of a fake food truck, and bar seating was sectioned off and clustered around the other stalls, mimicking the feel of restaurants, a dead institution. It made everything taste a little worse, coated as it was in longing, like the dust of the skybridges.

She got behind him in line at the "noodle" stall. Once she had her bowl, she made a show of looking for a seat before asking if she could take the one beside him. In Alice's experience, most people in the Mall disliked being interrupted from their bubbles of solitude or chosen company, even accidentally. She once asked the "muffin" vendor in basement six north what his favorite muffin was, and the deviation from script rattled his plastered smile into something like hatred.

But the Time Cube vendor looked terribly pleased, like he'd been expecting her. He had a wide mouth and thin lips that gave him a wolfish aspect when he grinned, and his hair was shiny and stiff with product. Alice had never cold-propositioned a stranger for sex, and she didn't know how to make the conversation move on from how much he enjoyed his nutritional patty, shredded into long, noodle-like strips. It turned out to be easy. She abruptly interrupted to ask if he had plans for the evening, and he did not.

Afterward, she tried to remember why her Depressive Specialist had recommended this. Had it lifted her mood? Alice had been demanding and straightforward; the Time Cube vendor was agreeable but self-involved, falling asleep after coming so easily and immediately it was like he'd been knocked out with a frying pan.

She got out of bed and wandered into the hall of his unit. He lived on west thirty. The lower floors of the west tower were older, the floor plans slightly larger but the ceilings lower, and because the mold-resistant coating was slathered on top of instead of woven into surfaces, the walls where her fingers brushed were grimy and damp. She'd spent so much time in her unit and identical ones that the small differences in square footage and height felt disorienting, the rooms elongated in perspective like a tunnel.

Incredibly, he had a second bedroom but no roommate, a fact that must have involved fraud or recent death. She thought the door to the second bedroom was locked, but she instinctively kept turning the handle and pushing the door with her shoulder, and discovered the lock was broken. With a pop, the door jerked suddenly open, the handle still stuck in the locked position, the faux wood juddering.

She closed the door behind her, forcing the handle a second time. She'd found what she was looking for, almost. The room was stuffed with machinery and tools, circuit boards, sheets of thick, uncut plastic. Workbenches lined three walls. A cylindrical machine, about eight feet long, took up most of the floor space, its top and bottom halves hinged together—a manufacturing mold for the cubes, perhaps.

Unfinished cubes were scattered on the benches and the floor, open-topped and missing their knobs. One was filled with gray ash. Another contained the bones of a bird lying on its side, pulled apart and picked nearly clean, just a few tufts of molding feathers along the back of one hip bone. Another had a rodent skeleton in a vivarium of living grass, a wraparound whip of bleached spine, skull, and front paws, the back legs missing. The sight of these tiny corpses, combined with the smell of sex clinging to Alice's skin, made her gut flop inside her like a swallowed fish. She could see why he stuck to selling the frog and plant versions.

She hadn't found a single finished Time Cube, a knob she could reel. Disappointment soured her tongue. In her search, she pulled out a latched case tucked under a workbench and flipped it open.

The case held an old, basic tablet computer, the kind commonly configured for single-purpose use—as a cash register, as a map, as a photo frame that rotated through pictures. It came to life in her hands and revealed itself as the latter. The photos were of an older man who closely resembled the Time Cube vendor, maybe his father or much older brother, all taken in casinos, strip clubs, concerts, raves, all dimly and colorfully lit. Drink glasses held aloft, attractive younger women surrounding him in bar booths and hot tubs. Fun as defined by an old beer commercial, or a certain kind of thirteen-year-old boy. As she scrolled, the teen-boy-at-heart developed liver spots on his bald pate, and bands of muscle and skin hung looser from the shrinking stem of his neck. All the background faces were smeared with alcohol, half-lidded or out of focus, but his eyes glowed with sober, consistent, childlike joy. He loved this life.

No weariness accompanied his aging. Alice wondered who he was to the Time Cube vendor, why this photo reel would be in his workshop. If his father was his hero or cautionary tale, or nothing to him at all.

She put the case back. She lifted the heavy lid of the machine she'd assumed was a manufacturing press, and was surprised to find that it was almost completely hollow on the inside. All of the machinery was pressed against the inner walls to accommodate the defined, empty space—wires and tubes and, bizarrely, metal gears, which Alice had only ever seen in textbooks when she was in school. The hollow was ovular, human-sized. Alice had trouble seeing the machine as she had before.

The inside of the upper lid had the same rotating knob as the Time Cubes.

Alice understood right away. She felt magnetically drawn, as she had been to the suicide-proof fencing on the skybridges, once, even as her thoughts were slow to form in words, to unspool the implications. She pressed one palm against the edge of the hollow for leverage as she swung her leg up and over to climb inside. She had to awkwardly hold up the heavy lid with the other hand to keep it from slamming shut on top of her limbs prematurely.

He'd chosen to make these silly toy cubes when he had the most sought-after power on earth, the stuff of poetry and legendary kings. He probably had the sense to know that his real product would make him hunted, rather than rich. Maybe he could have advertised it as an antiaging treatment, become secret cosmetic doctor to the stars, but even that would require letting people in too close. Better to use it only on himself, in the pettiest and most obvious way possible: to stay young and beautiful.

She let the lid settle over her. It didn't close completely—a thin edge of light was visible in the space between the two halves. She could hear herself breathing, and the ambient noise of the vendor's apartment, almost identical to the noise in her apartment, the gurgles and shuffling and thuds that were in everyone's walls, so heavily insulated from the outside and so thinly from one another.

She wondered what her Depressive Specialist would say. A healthy mind would want to turn the knob backward, hungry for more life, gasping for it, feeling the constriction of time like limited oxygen in a small room. A better person would grow philosophical. Maybe if she smashed open all the boxes, unraveled his machinery and ran the cords around the equator, she could spin the planet backward, go back far enough to save the world from itself.

But, Alice thought, she was as vain and self-obsessed as the Time Cube vendor, just in a different way. "Depressives are selfish," her Specialist had said. "You're selfish, and then you berate yourself for being selfish, which is just another way of focusing your attention on yourself." Said in the same gentle, infuriatingly patient voice in which she said everything.

Alice turned the knob to the right. Forward.

She thought she'd be focused on her body aging, like the plant and the frog, that she'd be able to feel, say, her hair graying and her teeth falling out and her wrinkles deepening, her muscles slackening, pain blooming in her joints, her sight and hearing fading. Or that she would die quickly, reach the clicking end of the knob and be released, let out through the door she had been pounding on for so long, the hum of existence finally quiet.

She hadn't wondered what the frog had been thinking, flying forward through his life, absorbing it all at once, the taste of every insect he would ever eat, everything those bulbous eyes would ever see. There was a rush that ruffled and stung like a strong wind. She hadn't anticipated a lifetime of joy and sorrow, beauty and mundanity and horror, all compressed into seconds. Entire arcs of romance and friendship with people she hadn't met yet, feeling the thrill of first connection at the same instant as their final betrayal. Her mouth kissed and her body entered and bruised thousands of times at once. Every Depressive nadir and reprieve, every greeting and goodbye, like being beaten across the face with a swinging door. Her nerves screamed, her spirit contorting through every action while her body lay still—except her fingers, still determinedly turning.

She heard, distantly, rustling elsewhere in the apartment. The Time Cube vendor opening the door to his bedroom. His footsteps pounding down the hall, his panicked voice incorrectly guessing her name. The broken lock popping free as he forced his way inside.

She turned the knob faster. Grief heaped upon her like dirt from a shovel, stacking and directionless. She mourned the loss of a beloved, as-yet-unknown person, simultaneously mourning the loss of dozens of others, a generation crumbling around her like pillars of salt. All of it spiraling around one emotion, one lesson, in tighter and tighter circles. That knowledge at the center—so near, almost within her grasp—kept her fingers turning, even as the Time Cube vendor tried to wrench the lid of the machine upward, as he kept shouting a name that wasn't her name. She held fast to the knob, listening for the click.

#CLIMBINGNATION

As April came in the door, she could immediately tell that the two magnetic poles of Travis's memorial were his older sister, Miki, and his climbing partner, Zach. Everyone gathered around one or the other. April recognized them both from Travis's Instagram. Miki sat with her feet up on the sofa in the living room that backed into the foyer, where she could both talk to the people sprawled at her feet on the rug and greet newcomers as they came through the front door, without getting up. She nodded at April as though they knew each other. Miki wore a black bodysuit and a patterned scarf the size of a beach blanket. The scarf was a riot of colors, and she held an end in each hand, so the fabric moved and fluttered around her as she gestured. Miki had a straight up-and-down body and long, elegant hands, amber eyes, and a triangular heap of curls that fell halfway down her back. She was appealing to look at, like a glazed cake.

Zach presided over the small kitchen, on the opposite end of the open-plan main floor. Casserole dishes and bottles of wine gathered on the counters. Zach wore gray technical shorts with oversized pockets and a plaid button-down, the sleeves rolled up and only the center two buttons done, so the tails flared out at the bottom and golden chest hair glinted over the top. He wasn't dressed appropriately, but who could blame him? Leaning back against the sink, he was appealing to look at in precisely the same way.

April beelined for the end of what amounted to a receiving line to talk to Zach. She found herself smiling, or grimacing, her mouth upturned involuntarily. "How awful," everyone said. "What a thing to witness. You must be a wreck. I'm so sorry. If you want to talk, I'm here." Their faces locked in those same smile-grimaces, as they patted him on the shoulder, the forearm. Lingering.

She looked out the window. The quiet street wound in wide curves, lined with trees, as in only the oldest, most expensive neighborhoods: cathedral-high elms touching canopy from opposite sides of the median, weeping beech sweeping their hair along the sidewalk, magnolias in full, pink bloom. Two teenage girls, standing at the end of the driveway, whispered in close conference, heads together, as though debating whether to go inside. They turned and stared back at April. She wondered if they'd also gotten the address from the obituary. Did teenagers even know about newspaper obituaries?

It was startling that the large room was filled with people her own age or younger, like a house party. She'd only been to funerals and memorials and wakes for elderly relatives—she had been lucky in that way. A bewildered widow or widower at the center, equally aged friends and siblings ringed tightly around them, oblivious small children running around the outside perimeter, April somewhere in between. Where, she wondered, were his parents, his aunts and uncles? When she pulled up outside, she'd assumed this house belonged to his parents; the two-story craftsman had an older, lived-in sensibility.

"I'm glad you weren't injured," the woman in front of April said, to Zach. "I mean, obviously I wish Travis had survived. I wish it hadn't happened at all! And of course it's the worst thing that could happen to a person, to you. I mean, not as bad as what happened to Travis. I mean, I'm just glad that you're physically—"

"I know what you meant," Zach said. "Thank you." He clasped her hand between both of his. As soon as he released his grip, she turned and fled from the room.

April knew it was an unfair thought, but up close, Zach did not look grief-stricken, like a haunted survivor. He had a healthy, well-rested glow. "I'm April," she said, stepping forward. "Travis and I were friends in college. I'm so sorry for your loss."

Zach studied her, and she felt caught in the lie. She and Travis had gone to the same college and lived in the same dorm building. In theory, they'd gone to the same parties, stood in the same rooms, but she couldn't remember if they'd ever actually met.

A few months earlier, he'd seemingly popped up on all her social media feeds at once: a tiny figure in an endless series of high-altitude landscapes, snowy fields above smokelike clouds, jagged cliffs piercing the sun. She'd been surprised to see that someone she'd plausibly known had five hundred thousand followers on Instagram, the population of a midsize city. She had no interest in mountaineering, yet she'd spent hours looking at close-ups of his knots, his blistered hands and shredded knuckles, his gear knolled on flat rocks. She'd watched hundreds of short videos of him leaping for a hold or pulling himself up a chimney, clicked "like" on hundreds of pictures of him posed hanging from a wall, or standing backlit and triumphant at the peak. One point four million thumbs up for his hypnotic charisma in a YouTube video. She gathered that he had only recently become popular, that everyone had found him at almost the same moment she did. The algorithm, mysterious as fate. He was less a person than a quilt of these beautifully colored squares. His view of the world from above, geographic and breathtaking, was so different from wherever she was: squatting over the toilet in her dark bathroom, lying in bed with a bag of unsalted tortilla chips balanced on her chest. He'd had the aura of a celebrity, and his sudden, violent death, his appearance in the mainstream news, felt perversely fitting. The famous should die famously.

"Thank you," Zach said.

"Can I ask . . ." April paused. "I understand if you don't want to talk about it, but I only know what I read in the news." She tried to soften her tone. "How did it happen?"

The news stories had been brief but vivid. Zach and Travis had been on a day climb in the North Cascades. A storm came in, and they wanted to get down quickly to avoid it. Something went wrong. Travis fell three hundred feet. The longest article that April had seen was padded out by embedded social media posts. Travis's last post, a selfie in the car with Zach, mugging with their tongues out, #climbingnation, flooded with comments and crying emojis. April added one that felt true enough—"I still can't believe it. You were an inspiration."—and felt a little thrill to see it pop up in the article, gathering hearts.

The room went silent. Miki craned her long neck in their direction.

Zach shook his head, his bangs falling into his eyes. He combed them back with his fingers. "It wasn't even forecasted to rain," he said. "It happened really fast. The wind picked up, the sky went dark. We knew we had to bail. We decided to do a simul-rappel. It's an emergency maneuver to get down fast, where you rappel down at the same time, using each other as a counterbalance."

Zach lifted his gaze. A rapt audience surrounded him. April noticed the teenage girls had come inside, hovering just past the threshold in the foyer. "One mistake, man. Travis made one mistake. The rope slipped through, and there was nothing I could do. He was just gone."

April could see it from Zach's perspective: the rocks darkened and slick in the rain. His muscles trembling with exhaustion as he held his body tight to the wall. A sudden, sickening loss of tension. Watching Travis fall, the loose coil of rope falling after him. Zach reaching out a futile hand, his scream drowned out in a roll of thunder. A lightning flash illuminating nothing, Travis too far below to see.

"And then what?"

April turned to the voice. Sitting in an armchair at Miki's side, the man who'd spoken looked like he'd come from the same mold as Zach and Travis: about the same age, with the same wiry build, deep tan, and shaggy hair. He wore a black suit over a T-shirt with no tie. "How did you get down and back to the car?" he said.

"I didn't," Zach said. "I waited on a ledge for help."

"You both fell, but there was a ledge on your side?"

"I didn't fall. I climbed down to the ledge."

"You were on the ledge when Travis fell? Like you'd gotten to the ledge first?"

"No, I climbed down to the ledge after Travis fell."

"Did the anchor fail?"

"Obviously not," Zach snapped. "I already said that he . . ." He wiped at his eyes. "You know what, Nick? I don't want to talk about this anymore."

April stepped closer to Zach. She rubbed him gently on the back. "At least Travis was doing something he loved," she said.

"He was," Zach said, sounding grateful. "He really was."

Nick exchanged a look with Miki, who shook her head with a slight smile, as though they were agreeing to indulge Zach on this. Nick's dark suit was a little too large for him. He sat slouched on the chair with his knees wide apart, the fabric pooling around him like a shadow.

Someone opened the unscreened windows, and the suburban noises, alien to April, joined the low din of the room: a screeching child's laugh, a bird singing incongruously into the evening. The hush of plants nestling against each other in the wind. The absence of cars. Miki turned on a floor lamp, still without getting up, and the circle of light around her seemed to grow brighter and more defined as it won its war of attrition against the sun.

The casseroles cooled and hardened. The wine bottles were emptied. When only a handful of people remained, April took it upon herself to start refilling everyone's glasses, opening a new bottle each time one was drained. The bottle opener was in the first drawer she tried, and she moved around the kitchen confidently, as though she knew it well.

She bent at the waist and reached diagonally across Zach's chest to pour red into his glass, her chest close to his chin where he sat. "April, you said, right? I don't think Travis ever mentioned you. You guys were close, back in the day?"

"You know how it is," she said. "We saw each other every day when we were in school, and then we fell out of touch. I always meant to reconnect. And then I missed my chance." She held the bottle against her body. Her eyes stung. How sad that would be, if it were true.

"Wow," he said. "To be honest, I was surprised there were so many people here. Travis was kind of a secretive guy, hard to get close to. I always thought he didn't have that many friends."

"Secretive?" April said. "He had half a million Instagram followers."

"Well, he was a climber and a photographer. That's not, like, actually knowing someone."

"He was secretive," Miki chimed in. Her voice was musical, regionless, and her mouth opened wide when she talked. April had once clicked through a tagged photo—@mikimikimiki, #siblinggoals—and seen, under her name and profile picture, the words *Theater Artist*. She waved at a group of people who were murmuring parting condolences as they left. One patted Miki on the shoulder awkwardly as he passed. Now April was alone with Miki, Zach, and Nick.

"He had a lot of strange ideas," Miki said, "but he knew he had to keep them to himself for the sake of his internet presence, business, whatever it was." She gestured with her empty wineglass. April sidled over with the bottle, pleased to be useful in this way, to blend in like the help. "Thank you, April."

"I did feel like he kept me at a distance," Zach said. "We'd drive and camp for days and days, but we mostly talked logistics and online shit."

"You put your lives in each other's hands," Miki said. "I can't imagine anything more intimate."

"That's just climbing. Sometimes you do that with people you just met." Zach shifted in his seat.

"You fuck people you just met, but if you keep fucking them, it becomes intimate all the same."

April put the bottle on the coffee table and slid in beside Miki on the couch, Nick on Miki's other side. "What kind of strange ideas?"

Miki twirled her scarf. "What was that?"

"You said Travis had a lot of strange ideas that he kept from his internet fans."

"Oh, you know, he was one of *those* people who thought the world was ending. Not in the biblical, street-preacher way. Climate change, peak oil. Global pandemic. That sort of thing."

"That's not so strange," Nick said. "Doesn't everyone feel that way by now?"

"But I could see how that wouldn't go with his internet persona," April said. Travis's blandly inspirational captions, the royalty-free rock music to which he set his videos, the continuous summits, peaks without valleys, had lately been the best diversion from the apocalyptic news.

"For Travis it went beyond that. He was prepared. Preparing." She looked around, meeting each of their eyes in turn.

Miki's thick, black eyebrows and eyelashes made her eyes burn a lighter brown, almost gold. She shrugged exaggeratedly and the wine sloshed in her glass. "I guess I can tell you all. It doesn't matter now."

She settled into the couch in a way that made her seem larger than before, her arms open, her chest expanded, the scarf pulled outward to either side. In the silence, April became aware that sometime in the last few minutes, the sun had dropped below the hard line of the horizon. All at once, it was night, the open windows portals to a depthless blue, the closed windows watery mirrors.

"He had a cabin," Miki said. "Not that far east along Highway Two, but deep in the bush, in the mountains. It was impossible to get to, on purpose. No roads. Days of bushwhacking, scrambling, free-climbing, river crossings. Completely inaccessible in the winter. High altitude. Functionally a fortress, surrounded by danger. I knew about it, but only he knew where it was. That is, until he died, and I got the deed to the land."

"Have you been?" April asked.

"I only just got the papers. And how would I get there? I could look into chartering a helicopter, I suppose, assuming there's somewhere to land."

"I find it hard to believe there's anywhere like that in the state that isn't either parkland or part of a reserve," Nick said.

"Believe what you like," Miki said. "That's how Travis described it, and I believe him. That's why he chose to build the cabin there."

"How did he even find the plot to buy in the first place?" Nick asked.

"I don't know," Miki said. She smoothed out a spot on her thigh where her bodysuit had ridden up and wrinkled. "I don't know, because when he told me about it, I was furious."

"Why?" April asked.

"Well, what does it say about who he planned to spend the end of the world with? Certainly not me. I'd never make it. Either he meant to go it alone, or . . ." Miki gestured at Nick and then Zach. "Or with his adventuring buddies."

"He never mentioned it to us," Zach said, quietly.

Nick continued to press. "If it's so hard to access, how did he construct the cabin? How did he get the materials and tradespeople there?"

"According to the documents, it's more like a shack," Miki said. "And he built it himself. As for how he got the materials there, I would guess—piece by piece."

April pictured Travis free-climbing with a bundle of two-by-fours strapped to his back. That part, if nothing else, fit into his internet aesthetic.

"I suppose I will have to go eventually," Miki went on. "It'd be a shame to let all the supplies go to waste."

"He was already keeping it stocked?" April asked.

Miki nodded. "He could only schlep so much in at one time, but I think at this point there's quite a lot of shelf-stable food, fuel, and water. And he was installing a gravity pump, I remember."

"There was a water source even higher up than the cabin?" Nick said.

Miki waved one end of the scarf. "Nick, I only know what Travis told me. I only learned where this place even is in the last couple days."

"I'm amazed you got the deed already," April said. "When my great-aunt died, the bureaucracy of it all took forever."

"Travis had a will," Miki said. "He'd update it before he went on any big adventure trip, particularly overseas. Ironic that he died on a day climb practically in his backyard." Throughout the conversation, Miki's tone had been droll, almost amused, dry of grief. She stared into the middle distance. "Maybe I'll let the place rot up there. In a thousand years, an archaeologist can puzzle over it, all the gold."

"Gold?" they chorused.

Miki laughed. "I told you, he was one of those people. He thought only gold would be worth anything in the new world order. I know he was regularly buying one-ounce bars from a place on the Eastside and stashing them in the cabin."

Nick was already looking it up on his phone. "Right now, an ounce of gold is worth about twelve hundred dollars."

Miki's features were large, cartoonishly expressive. She could lift her eyebrows almost to her hairline. "Good Lord. Well, no wonder he had almost nothing in the bank." She stretched in her seat. "I guess I will have to go to the cabin after all. That's too much money to leave for future archaeologists."

Nick shook his head. "This just doesn't sound like Travis to me. He was the most optimistic person I knew."

"There's optimism in being prepared," Miki said.

"And I thought he was a big believer in never even hiking alone. Safety in numbers and all that. I can't imagine him bushwhacking, solo, to his fortress of gold."

"Death," Miki began, seemingly pausing for effect, "has a way of unveiling the truth. But as you said, Travis was many things. Let's talk about some of the others. April, I would love to hear what he was like in college."

"Oh." April put her glass on the table and topped it up. "Nick, Zach, did you guys know him then?"

Zach shook his head. He hadn't spoken in a while, and his expression was distant, faintly disturbed. "We met after, when we were all working at the same ski resort."

"How about you, Miki? Were you in close contact?"

"No, not really. Travis and I were close growing up, and later when I moved back, right up until he died." Miki's voice continued to strike April as strange, overenunciated, with a perpetual note of irony. "But we lost touch a bit when he was in college. I was living in LA, and my life was busy, and not terribly pleasant."

April sipped her wine and considered. "Everybody loved him," she said, finally. "He was funny, and he had a way of addressing a room full of people and making it feel like he was only talking to you. Girls would leave little Post-it Notes on his dorm room door." She was thinking of his vlogs and their comment sections.

Miki seemed to waver for the first time. She laughed again, softer, more bitterly. "That sounds right."

April wasn't sure when she'd fallen asleep, but she woke up and Nick and Miki were also out, the three of them huddled together on the couch. Zach wasn't in the room. April padded down the hall, her dry lips crusted violet from the wine, looking for a bathroom.

Coming around the corner, she could see into a study through the glass panels of its French doors. The lamp on the desk was on, its head downcast, blasting the tabletop with a startlingly bright, yellow light in the otherwise dark room. She heard the artificial shutter sound of a phone camera. It took her a moment to see Zach bent over the desk, taking photos of the papers arranged there.

The bathroom was before the study, along the same wall. She ducked in to use it, and then rejoined the others in the living room. Zach had not returned. She curled back up against Miki, who stirred but didn't wake.

Zach came back in a few minutes later. He gently shook Miki by the arm. "Miki? I'm going to go."

She grabbed on to his wrist without opening her eyes. "Let's stay in touch, okay?"

"Of course."

Nick wasn't fully awake until the front door had opened and closed. "Did Zach leave?"

Miki made a noise of assent.

Nick exhaled a long breath. "I feel bad for him. I really do. It's the kind of mistake anyone could make, and to be responsible for your best friend's death . . . That's devastating. Unbelievably devastating. But his denial is fucked up."

Miki removed her scarf, which she had been using as a blanket, and draped it over the top of the couch. It had become a part of her body in April's mind. It was like watching Miki pop her arm from its socket, or strip off her skin. Though the bodysuit went almost to her ankles, the material was thin and stretched to translucence. "It doesn't matter. Travis is gone either way."

"It doesn't bother you? Having him blame Travis?"

Miki started gathering up the glasses. April rose to help her. "Whatever he has to tell himself to get through, I understand."

"How do you know he's lying?" April said.

Nick looked at Miki, who nodded. "There aren't that many ways that only one person falls from a simul-rap," he said. "Zach must have lost control of the brake and not tied an end-stop knot. It sounds to me like he got to a ledge and just unweighted without thinking—took his weight off the rope—as you usually do when you touch ground rappelling. So the rope slid through his device, there was no time to grab it, no knot at the end . . ." Nick rubbed his face. His cheeks were flushed from the alcohol and creased from sleep. "I'm just speculating, but I can't think of a way Travis could have made a mistake that led to his own fall in that setup. If Travis had fucked up, either they both would have fallen, or just Zach."

Miki and April put the glasses by the sink. Without asking, April put the stopper in the drain and started to fill one basin with hot water and soap.

"I wish I could be as understanding as you, Miki," Nick said. "I can barely look at him." He ran a hand through his floppy bangs, the same gesture Zach had made earlier, through the same haircut. April had seen Travis do the same thing while speaking directly to the camera held in his other hand. "I know it was an accident, but I blame him. It's his fault that Travis is gone. I want to grab him and shake him and ask how he could forget to tie a fucking knot. It'd be easier if he just admitted it. I think I could forgive him then. But now, now it feels . . ." Nick's voice cracked.

Miki left April to wash the glasses. She came and folded Nick into her arms. She was only a hair taller than him, but her long limbs and the way he shrank and crumbled in the embrace made them resemble a mother and child. "Nick," she said, speaking into his hair, "why don't you go home and go to sleep? We're all going to be dealing with this for a long time. One day at a time, okay?"

Nick nodded. He swiped at his eyes as he and Miki pulled apart. He paused at the front door in his rumpled suit and said, "It was nice to meet you, April. I wish it could have been under better circumstances."

April nodded, unable to speak. The door clicked shut.

Miki walked the perimeter of the room, turning on all the lights, closing the windows, lowering the blinds. April set the wineglasses in the rack to dry and started rooting around in the drawers for plastic wrap to cover the mummified casseroles.

"It's so kind of you to stay and clean up when no one else did," Miki said. "Leaving me to grieve in a messy house. Some friends."

"I have to tell you something."

"Oh?"

"I saw Zach, earlier. While you were asleep. In the study. Taking pictures of some papers with his phone. I'm going to guess they were—related to the cabin."

Miki turned and tugged on the cord to lower the last set of blinds. She was silent for a long moment. Finally, she said, "Did you notice those two teenage girls today?"

"What? Did you hear what I said about Zach?"

"The girls arrived at about the same time you did. When I asked them who they were, they admitted they were just fans of Travis online. They'd never met him. At first, I was going to ask them to leave, but then I thought, who was I to say they didn't know him just as well as any of us? Zach didn't know Travis enough to say whether or not he was a doomsday prepper. And Zach was the one who got him killed."

April put down the box of plastic wrap. Her gaze darted to the front door.

"Strangers loved my brother, and I have hundreds— thousands—of pictures and videos to remember him by. That's kind of beautiful, in its way." Miki was still staring at the covered window, the dusty vinyl an inch from her face. "It's a crazy story, isn't it?"

"How Travis died?"

"No. Well, that too. But I meant the cabin. A hidden trove of gold, where only the most skilled mountaineer can reach it! A treasure map left in plain sight, when you can just download templates for wills and deeds off the internet. It's like something out of a children's book. Knowing Zach, he probably started packing a gear bag the second he got home, not wanting me and my helicopter to beat him." Miki laughed. "Nick was driving me nuts with all those questions. 'How did Travis find it? How did he build? How could a place like that exist in this state?'"

The wine felt like a dying animal in April's gut, and the embedded ceiling lights Miki had turned on were queasily bright. April edged out of the kitchen, toward Miki and the door beyond. She was only just beginning to understand. "Does it?"

"Of course. There's plenty of high, remote places, that would take days or weeks of backpacking to get to, surrounded by terrain that could easily maim or kill you in the approach. Especially if you were expecting a big cache of supplies and water when you got there." Miki finally turned. Pinprick reflections in her eyes glittered like stars. "Are you leaving?" she asked abruptly, seeing April standing in the middle of the room.

"I . . . Yes. I'm sorry again for your loss."

Miki showed her teeth, her mouth twisted to the side, somewhere between a grin and a sneer. "Didn't you lose him too?"

Miki stayed where she was, leaving April to see herself out. She didn't have a coat. April closed the door behind her. She hadn't realized she'd been holding her breath until she let it out on their front stoop, suddenly gulping air. This neighborhood had fewer streetlights than hers, and besides the one she'd just left, all of the houses were dark. Zach and Nick were long gone, no sign of anyone on the sidewalk.

In her car, she took out her phone. Her battery was almost dead. All of Travis's accounts had been deleted or changed to private, sometime that day, a large error block in the news articles where the embedded posts had been. As had Miki's. Without them, she couldn't think of a way to connect to Zach. His last name, in the articles, was uselessly common, and she couldn't remember his handles. She did not, in fact, know these people at all. She imagined trying to explain this to the police, that Zach might die trying to steal something that didn't exist. She didn't know where Miki had sent him, where they should look. She imagined a skeptical officer sitting across from her, in the middle of the night, in the station for this sleepy, wealthy suburb. Middle-aged but still getting the graveyard shift, the skin of his face puffy and cracked like overrisen cake, someone peripherally aware of Instagram and YouTube as something his children did. And who are you, he'd ask. Who are you to them?

SANDMAN

The person sitting at the end of Kelly's bed wore a gray, hooded cloak. The hood hung over his forehead and drooped across his shoulders in an elongated oval, his unseen face recessed in the depths of the fabric. The hem covered his feet, even in his seated position, and wide bell sleeves covered his hands to the fingertips. One shrouded hand rested on her shin. Kelly was not afraid. The way he sat—his knees and hips facing out over the side of the bed, his torso turned toward her, his hand low on her leg—seemed parental, benevolent.

Monsters rarely figured in Kelly's dreams. In her most frequently recurring dream, she was lost in a large building, looking for a specific room among hallways of endless doors. For most of her life, it had been an infinite, shifting school; recently it had become an infinite, shifting hotel, hosting a conference.

The figure climbed onto Kelly's bed on his hands and knees. He traveled up her body until his face—where his face would be—hovered over hers. He held himself up with his hands by her head, every inch of him covered by the puddling fabric. In the darkened room, she stared into the featureless hole at the center of his hood. He carried the metallic scent of someone who had just come in from outside in the winter.

A trickle of sand touched her lower lip. Sand poured out from within his hood, in a thin, continuous stream. She parted her lips, opened her throat as if to sing. She still couldn't see his face, but she sensed that the sand was traveling from his mouth and into hers, the matte-gold dust glowing dully, catching the faint light that leaked around her drawn curtains.

The sand flowed faster. She felt the grains coursing down her throat, entering her abdomen, entering a cavity she hadn't known was there, a cathedral emptiness where her organs should have been. She swallowed without gagging, almost without breathing. The sand filled her, weighing her down. She could feel the sand spreading, swelling her belly and traveling into her limbs, pinning her body slowly to the mattress, too heavy to lift under her own power. She had never felt so full, so satisfied.

The longest Kelly had ever gone without sleeping was four days and three nights, when she was thirteen. The details were fuzzy to her now. She remembered that she had begun to hallucinate bugs at the periphery of her vision, white moths and sparkling, winged beetles dancing along her hairline and jaw, and she knew that the streak ended with a visit to the pediatrician. Yet she couldn't recall talking to her parents about her insomnia—not then, not ever. She remembered the doctor saying she wasn't getting enough exercise and stimulation during the day; she must be sitting around idle, watching too much TV, eating too much sugar. A friend of Kelly's, a doctor herself, later told her that sleeping pills were almost never prescribed to children, then or now, but Kelly vividly remembered the pills she took: round and yellow, with a rectangular notch across the middle, as though to fit a very fine screwdriver.

Kelly no longer thought of her insomnia as remarkable or pathological. Her friends who had children often complained of their "problem sleepers"—the elaborate bedtime routines, the seven-year-olds still in their parents' beds, the songs and books and glasses of water and white-noise-producing, vibrating, oscillating gadgets. Kelly's parents had locked their bedroom door at night. As a child, Kelly had frequently climbed out of bed to wait for morning in the hallway outside her parents' room. She'd start out sitting or kneeling and eventually slide to the floor, lying on her side with the cool linoleum against her cheek. She'd wake there, the narrow windows framing gray predawn light, her neck kinked from the hard floor, and hurry back to her room before her parents got up.

In college, everyone stayed up all night to party or to cram. She'd look up from her library carrel in the small hours of the morning and see her fellow students wandering by in pajamas. She'd spent the nights before a project was due in a twenty-four-hour café, ordering a double espresso every two hours, watching the barista wilt and disappear into the back for covert naps, his eyes reddened and shadowed in tandem with hers. She was often the last one awake at the end of a house party, alone with the full force of daylight on a fire escape.

Now, in adulthood, everyone complained about not sleeping enough, not sleeping well. They stayed up to work, they stayed up to worry, the baby kept them up, they got caught up in a TV show or fell down an internet rabbit hole, who could rest in these troubled times? In her twenties, Kelly had had bursts of middle-of-the-night productivity, where she scrubbed the overlooked crevices of her apartment—the tops of the baseboards, the ice trays, the overflow drain in the bathroom sink—or cooked large batches of soup, reorganized her closets. In her thirties, these spikes of energy faded, but sleep didn't replace them. She just rolled over to the side of the bed and reached for her phone, the portal of light that made the room around her disappear, the articles and videos and jokey, self-deprecating reassurance that millions of others were doing the same. When she went to the doctor, she ticked off "trouble falling asleep" and "trouble staying asleep" on the check-in form, but it was never the reason she'd come, and her doctor never mentioned it.

These unbroken stretches of consciousness, days sometimes blurring into one another, seemed just a feature of modern life, not worth complaining about.

A week before her first visit from the man in the cloak, as Kelly was getting coffee from the break room, her coworker Thibault came in and asked, "Did you sleep well?" as a greeting. Thibault was originally from Belgium and retained an accent. His job title was one level below hers, on a team that worked with the one Kelly managed. Not her direct subordinate, technically. He had wispy blond hair and large, shallow-set blue eyes, and the broad-boned, sunken, two-dimensional look of someone too lean for his frame. In a vague, lackadaisical way, Kelly wanted to sleep with him.

She answered honestly, in her calibrated office-small-talk voice. "No, not really. But that's not unusual. I'm not a great sleeper."

Thibault lit up. "How's your sleep hygiene?"

Everyone else in the office found him tedious. They dreaded hearing why he was putting butter in his coffee or why his latest cleanse had lent him a sickly, herbaceous smell. His schemes and diets seemed, to Kelly, driven by a misguided belief in the perfectibility of the human body. His dumb optimism made it impossible to imagine him fucking, to imagine a shadow of brutality crossing his face, that any part of him wanted to split another person in half. It felt like a challenge.

"My what?" She stirred her coffee longer than necessary.

"The things you do to improve your sleep quality." He sounded pleased she didn't know the term. He reeled off a list of prescriptions: sunlight, an empty bedroom used only for sleep, no caffeine past noon. "Like everything else," he concluded, "it's about trying to live the way we were evolved to, back in our caveman days. I'll send you some links!"

When she next saw Thibault that week, he asked if she'd read the articles he'd emailed her, and she lied that she hadn't yet. Showering at night, trying to find time during the day to go outside, eating an earlier dinner, not bringing her phone and laptop and snacks into bed with her, removing all traces of work and clutter from her bedroom, laundering her gritty sheets, hanging blackout curtains, giving up her afternoon coffee—it seemed like a lot. Thibault's manager overheard, and later, when they crossed paths in the ladies' room, asked if Kelly wanted her to intervene. "You can't give that health nut an in," she said, in a tone that was only half-teasing. "He'll never let up."

Kelly was slow to answer. "I am tired, though."

"We're all tired."

That Saturday, Kelly sat in one of the dented, unused chairs in the overgrown courtyard of her apartment complex, her head throbbing with caffeine withdrawal. She closed her eyes as the sun hit her face, forcing herself to stay awake—no naps allowed. In the evening, she took a picture of her emptied bedroom from the perspective of her clean, neatly made bed, one of her bare and freshly showered legs at the edge of the frame. She'd done everything except the blackout curtains. She texted the picture to Thibault, hoping it came off as flirty but indistinct.

He texted back, "Good for you!!! Sleep well!!!"

She plugged in her phone in the kitchen, out of reach. As usual, once she turned off the light and crawled under the covers, she felt the muscles in her face and back tightening, snapping alert. As usual, the room felt bright, the snow-white duvet cover aglow, and she longed for her phone. She tucked her fingers into the boxer shorts she slept in and got herself off in a few minutes, her mind blank, unable to fantasize about anything in particular, and felt no more relaxed. She closed her eyes, counting the seconds, her thoughts interrupting and jumbling the numbers.

When she opened her eyes, the man in the cloak was there.

Afterward, after he'd filled her, after he'd rearranged her internal workings and made her swell and buried her from the inside, she discovered that it was late the next morning. She'd been in bed for fourteen hours straight.

For the first few hours of her day, Kelly felt both sharpened and dazed, her spine lengthened, her eyelids pulled back, the contrast on the world turned up, black shadows and startling edges to every surface. Her feet felt in looser contact with the floor, a floating ballerina brush-step as she walked, her neck a loose, springy tether on her head's helium drift. Her face looked different in the mirror—younger, wide-eyed. Credulous and undamaged.

She had lunch with Gillian, a friend from college she rarely saw, as they lived in different boroughs with an infrequent bus between them. She showed Gillian the picture of Thibault from her company's online directory. Gillian's nose squished up in distaste. Kelly expected Gillian to say that she didn't think he was cute, but a more disturbing phrasing rolled out: "Is this really your best option? Is this the best of the men you know?"

"I'm not marrying him," Kelly said. "I'm not even dating him. It's just a work crush."

"It's a waste of energy," Gillian said. She looked closer at the photo on Kelly's phone. "He kind of looks like Brendon."

Brendon had been Kelly's college boyfriend. He could be described in the same broad strokes as Thibault: slim, sandy-haired, blue-eyed. But unlike Thibault, Brendon had been unequivocally, conventionally beautiful, in the manner of a teen idol—delicate features, long eyelashes, large white teeth.

When Kelly thought of Brendon, she pictured him asleep. He'd slept deeply and easily, snoring the moment the lights went out. Asleep through fire engine sirens, through jackhammers and leaf blowers, through neighbors' radios and drum kits and dogs. Through heat waves, as Kelly sweated and thrashed beside him, as Kelly got up and left the room, as she jangled her keys and clomped around in her shoes and banged shut the front door and went to wander the empty streets. His jaw slack and a small, tender smile on his lips. Kelly had spent many hours watching him sleep, directing the fury of her wakefulness in his direction, willing him to join her in the hot, noisy, agitating realm of the conscious.

Kelly virtuously refused the end-of-meal coffee she wanted and parted ways with Gillian. On the way home, she bought cheap polyester blackout curtains and a pair of fabric shears. After she'd cut them to size and attached them to her existing curtains, she stood back to admire her efforts. She considered sending another picture to Thibault. Gillian's question troubled her. *The best of the men you know.* Like Kelly should put all the single men she knew into bracketed tiers until only one remained, worthy of her love. More distressing was the thought that Thibault might actually *be* the best of them. He meant well, he took care of himself, he had that accent. She didn't text.

She slept in the nude that night, moving quickly from the warm steam of another nighttime shower through her bedroom to slide under the weight of the duvet. She had almost forgotten about the new curtains, and when she tugged the pull-cord on her bedside lamp, the purity of the darkness startled her. She couldn't see her own arms as she extended them in front of her. She had to trust a kinesthetic sense of where they were, that they remained attached to her. Her palms and the pads of her fingers tingled, as though she were standing on a high cliff and looking down. The dark seemed to have substance, a pudding-like resistance that slowed the movement of her invisible arms. When she pulled the duvet back, the darkness seemed to descend upon her, cool to the touch, making her conscious of the highest peaks of her body: the tip of her nose, her toes, her upturned nipples.

Lying dead center on the mattress, Kelly could neither see nor reach any edge of the bed, like it went on forever. She lay surrounded by empty, eternal, starless space.

She felt him in the room with her.

The skirt of the cloak brushed against her bare legs, the fabric heavy but soft. As he had the previous night, he hovered above her, his hands out to the side, not touching her. There was a long, suspended moment where he might have been observing her, except there was nothing to see and nothing to do the seeing—no eyes shone in the cavernous hood, both of their forms submerged in the dark.

She parted her lips and exhaled a purposeful stream, like she was trying to cool a cup of tea. It was the only way she could think to ask for what she wanted. This time, he lowered his face onto hers, the hood coming down around her ears and the top of her head, enclosing her in a smaller, closer, even richer darkness. A kiss, at first not unlike any other good kiss. Then she opened, as she had the night before, widening inside her throat, her chest, her gut, her pelvis. That sensation of being enormous and hollow on the inside, as though she contained acres of open field under a prairie sky, as though she contained a cenote that descended to the center of the earth.

Deep in their kiss, the sand flowed from his throat and down hers. She moved around experimentally, as more and more of her body became immobilized: first her core grew leaden, then she could no longer move her limbs, then her twiddling fingers and toes ceased. Lastly her mind. The sweep of sand like a veil draped over her mind, her thoughts dissolving into wordlessness, an inner silence as total as the darkness of the room.

The spritely, elongated feeling lasted longer the next day, until almost two p.m. When she felt it fading, she went to buy a coffee from the cart downstairs, in the office lobby, breaking the rule against afternoon caffeine. She was determined to finish the documentation she'd been working on. She brought her work laptop home and gave up around midnight. She hadn't bothered to turn on the lights as the daylight had faded, and her living room was now illuminated only by the computer screen. She rubbed her strained eyes and the afterimage of text and figures swam across her vision.

She streamed reruns of a 1980s sitcom on her TV. As she lay on her side on the couch, the speckled image and spackled makeup and canned laughter were like landscape passing through a car window. She thought of the man in the cloak, imagined her body heavy and powerless, and under her strumming fingers she came as she hadn't in years, ropes of electricity whip-cracking through her.

She returned to the report and wrapped it up quickly, a little shoddily, emailing it to her team at three in the morning. Some of them would be awoken by the vibration of their phones, the demanding growl as the devices convulsed in place. They would mutter about it to their partners, in bed beside them, and to one another the next day: Kelly is always working, Kelly doesn't sleep, Kelly doesn't have a life, does she expect the same of us? Kelly hit the send button and sent a ripple of anxiety and spite out into the city, into the night. She felt better. She put the TV show back on and dozed, the volume low, so familiar she could almost see it through her eyelids. Morning light replaced it, penetrating the thin layer of flesh, the backlit blood vessels glowing pink.

The next night—Tuesday—Kelly went to her twenty-four-hour gym at two a.m., empty save for a janitor pushing his vacuum between the machines. She slept on a recumbent bicycle while still pedaling, the resistance at zero, her legs spinning free and her head lolling. A cable news anchor barked from a hanging TV overhead.

On Wednesday, after work, she napped in her apartment building's courtyard, sleep with the texture of tattered lace, frayed threads of dream woven into reality's edge. She noticed a neighbor watching her from his window. She waved.

On Thursday evening, she gathered all the food wrappers and papers and mostly empty bottles and unread books and dirty clothes that had gathered in and around her bed, as though they'd washed up there in the tide, and tossed them onto the kitchen table for later sorting. She re-tucked the sheet corner that had come loose, shook the dust and crumbs out of the duvet, changed the pillowcases. She vacuumed. She drank a chamomile tea. She left her phone in the kitchen again, face-down. She did a series of stretches on the floor. She took a hot shower. She drew the blackout curtains and tucked herself in.

The man in the cloak didn't come.

Once Friday morning had firmly arrived, Kelly went to an all-night diner. She ordered fried eggs, bacon, sausage, hash browns, white toast. She curled up in the booth, her feet tucked under her on the bench and her head pushed into the corner between the booth and the wall. Her eyes closed, she listened to the scrape of cutlery on plates, the hiss of the flattop grill. The waitress shook her shoulder, not unkindly. "You can't sleep here," she said. Kelly nodded. She ate everything, cutting it into small cubes, chewing each one at length, drawing out the meal as it consumed the last of the night, the bites turned lukewarm and rubbery. Her dozen refills of coffee seared in her gut as she left for work. By the diner wall clock, shaped like a sunburst, it wasn't quite seven.

Thibault stood alone at the bank of elevators as she came in, still in his comical-looking biking gear: helmet, fingerless gloves, skintight jersey and shorts, the melon-bulge of his calves and crotch. They hadn't spoken since the week before. She steeled herself for another cheery conversation about her sleep habits, the text she'd sent.

Thibault looked uncommonly lost in thought, and he didn't notice her until she was right beside him. They both said hello, the *o*'s drooping and lost, like there wasn't enough air in the room. He was visibly sweaty, but her own smell was stronger, the diner coffee gone even more acrid.

"You're still not sleeping well," he said.

She shook her head.

"And you tried . . ." He went through all the things she'd done the day before and she confirmed each one, until he reached things she hadn't. Giving up caffeine entirely. Giving up sugar, meat, dairy, alcohol. Meditation, hypnosis, acupuncture, massage, nasal rinsing, tinted lenses, melanin. How much cardiovascular exercise did she get in a week? There was a conscious relaxation app he could send her. And she shouldn't expect it to work all the time, right away. It might take weeks or months of consistent—

"Fucking ridiculous," Kelly said. Her voice was low and clipped, almost a whisper.

"What?"

"Working this hard at relaxing. Turning *rest* into *work*. Making it stressful, making it a competition, another way you can feel like you're better than everyone else. Can't you see how absurd that is?"

Thibault rubbed his hand along the side of his bike shorts, a seemingly unconscious gesture, the slick spandex stretched over his sinewy thigh. "I don't think I'm better than you," he said. "I was just trying to help."

The elevator pinged, opened, swallowed them. In the brushed steel of the elevator doors, she could see their warped, impressionistic reflections, two smudges of color.

Moving slowly, as though through water, Thibault reached toward her. He cupped her face with one hand, turning it toward him. His thumb stroked the curve of bone at the bottom of her eye socket, slid down over the puffy, bruise-violet skin, his gaze following.

The elevator pinged their arrival. He stepped back. She waited for him to speak. When he didn't, she strode out the elevator doors, already starting to close.

The following week, Kelly, the other managers, and a selection of senior employees went to a two-day seminar at their corporate headquarters in Indianapolis. Her hotel room, otherwise unremarkable, was freezing, cold air blasting from an unidentified source despite the tepid weather. She fiddled with the digital thermostat, turning it up and changing the modes to no effect. No one answered the phone at the front desk. She took all the extra bedding out of the closet, piled it onto the bed, and burrowed underneath, her socks still on, her knees curled into her chest.

She alternated between tucking her head under the heap to warm her nose and cheeks and coming up again for air. She'd arrived at the airport too early for the short flight and had had to endure hours of chitchat with her colleagues. Then a group dinner, where she'd nursed a single glass of white wine and maintained a bland, thin-lipped smile. The beige furniture and beige walls of her hotel room, punctuated only by a single two-toned color-block painting, were a relief.

Her fingers caught at fabric that differed from the rough coverlet and scratchy sheets and spongy, fire-retardant blankets. She pulled the fabric toward herself. She knew by feel that it was the cloak. He was lying behind and beside her, one arm wrapped around her waist.

She reached into the sleeve and felt for his hand and forearm, surprised to find it was just that—five fingers, a veiny wrist, and the tender depression at the inside of his elbow. She wasn't sure what she had expected. A skeleton, a claw, the featureless flipper of a dolphin. She realized then what she'd hoped for: an empty cloak, held up by spectral magic. A bodiless force. She drew her hands back.

They lay together in a bubble of space, the blankets tented overhead by unseen supports, a dome-like roof she could sense but not see. Without touching her skin, he lifted off her loose nightshirt. She rolled and settled on her back. She opened and closed her eyes and found there was no difference. She couldn't see anything at all, no shadows or the suggestion of motion, no variations in the darkness.

She felt sand trickling across her right arm, accumulating slowly, each pinpoint as barely perceptible as a snowflake. This was new: he was burying her arm from the outside, an increasing mound of sand that left her hand and shoulder exposed. The sand had a nighttime cool, the faintest suggestion of damp. He moved to the other arm. He was precise, few grains straying from the tight pack around her arms.

More sand, poured at a faster clip, blanketed her feet and her shins. A heavy collar of sand pressed down on her throat. She was like an animal with markings that show where it's the most vulnerable, her face and underbelly left exposed to the air as the rest of her disappeared.

The hotel bed was no longer at her back, the pillow no longer cradling her head. She was lying on a stretch of sand, a midnight desert. She was sinking. She let her hands fall, slip under. She relaxed her shoulders and felt them vanish. The sand made a soft, shushing sound as it gathered, as hillocks formed and collapsed. Soon she was craning her head back, just her face floating above the surface of the dunes. His kiss descended on her, the same comforting, crushing pressure of the sand that surrounded her, and she was gone.

Kelly sat up in bed. Past her hotel window, dawn rose over the clustered skyline, the sun doubled on the canal running through downtown. She could hear stirring in a neighboring room, water

77

in pipes, twittering birds on the concrete sill. She looked at the bulky armoire in the corner, stern-looking wood with a reddish finish, and felt a sudden conviction that she could lift it. She could lift anything in the room. She felt superhuman.

In the T-shirt and sweatpants she'd slept in, her card key tucked in the waistband and her feet bare, she stepped into the hallway. She knocked on the door she knew was Thibault's. With the same heightened clarity, like it was a movie she'd seen many times before, she envisioned herself pushing past him and into the room, crowding him to the edge of the bed, shoving him onto his back, stripping them both while he gaped, straddling him and fucking him senseless, not a word exchanged.

It was a long time before she heard footfalls on his side of the door. A pause while he must have been looking at her through the peephole. He opened the door a crack, then pulled it back and stepped into the gap so they could face each other.

She started forward and he held out a hand, level with her shoulder, stopping her. He shook his head, his eyes downcast and his lips slightly curled, an expression of pity, politeness, gratitude-but. He held the handle as he let the door shut again, slowing its swing so the closure was almost soundless.

Kelly stood there, stunned. A door opening down the hall finally sprung her into motion and she scurried back to her room.

The man in the cloak didn't return for nearly a month. Day bled into night into day. She slept in a bathroom stall at work. She slept on the bus. She slept while getting her hair cut. She slept during conversations. She slept upright with her eyes open at her desk. At best, she slept for the first or last couple hours of the night. None of it was sleep, exactly—she could perceive how much time was passing or when the bus was nearing her stop; she could appear to be listening and catch the gist of what was being said. She lost small shards of time, a few seconds or less, the film reel of the world stuttering forward.

One night, she walked to a movie theater across town that had midnight showings of old movies on weekdays. She settled into a seat at the back, upholstered in worn green velvet, her feet sore from the hour-long walk in flats. The movie that night was *Singin' in the Rain*, and before the opening credits were over, the loud, jaunty orchestration and yellow typeface over umbrellas, her eyes fluttered shut.

When she opened them, the theater was empty, and her first thought was that she'd slept through the whole film. Except the house lights remained off, and the screen was still glowing without a picture, just a lit gray rectangle.

The man in the cloak sat in the seat beside her, his sleeve spilling over the armrest.

She spoke directly into the sagging, empty hood. "Why am I like this?" she said. "Why don't you come to me every night, like you do everyone else?"

She reached inside his sleeve to take his hand. Her fingers found only a loose configuration of sand. She recoiled. A thin, anemic stream of sand ran out onto the floor.

Above them, the glass of the projection booth shattered, an explosive change in pressure. The booth had been filled with sand, now gushing down onto their heads through the hole. Sand burst open all the theater doors, front and back.

Waves of sand as high as the doorframes cascaded down the aisles, piled up over the seats, higher and higher. She jumped out of her seat. The sand was up to her knees, too yielding to run on, making her stumble as she tried to escape. Up to her waist in an instant, the theater filling fast, corner to corner.

The empty cloak floated by on a current of incoming sand, flat as a paper doll.

She clawed and fought and tried to stay above it, in the vanishing air, trying to protect her stinging eyes, the sand coating her mouth, sucking the moisture from her. The doorframes burst, the walls caved in. The world beyond the theater was made entirely of sand, eager to occupy the void. A torrent of sand knocked her sideways. She was quickly covered under a choking, scraping blanket of darkness.

Kelly opened her eyes. Everything was quiet and still. She was back in the desert, but this time she could see: undulating dunes stretched in all directions, curves snaking to the horizon. The sky was an unnatural color, a collision of blues, indigo and electric, emanating a flat light absent sun, moon, or stars. She was sitting upright and naked in a wide, high-backed chair sculpted from sand. A throne, decorated in an intricate pattern of whorls. She picked up a handful of sand and let it run through her fingers, the texture unnervingly different from before—powdery as flour, no grit.

She realized the man in the cloak was sitting at her feet, facing away from her, his back against the base of the throne. His head—through the hood—leaned lightly against her knee.

When he spoke, his voice seemed to come from all around her, from nowhere in particular, directly into her mind.

Do you think, he said, I come to everyone the way I come to you?

He rose to his feet, turning around, like a column of sand rising out of the ground before her. The cloak sleeves settled over her hands and arms, facing up on the armrests of her throne. His hidden hands cinched around her wrists and locked them in place.

He leaned forward. A pinch of sand sprinkled across her brow, sparkly as craft-store glitter. She blinked it away. He released her wrists and stood upright again, turned as if to leave. And she understood, though he was silent: There, now you're like everyone else.

The hood was angled over his shoulder, as though he were looking back at her, expecting her to call him back, to beg for his occasional, ecstatic visits between long seasons of wakefulness. To keep her secret knowledge of the workings of the universe, of every hour of the night, the changing shadows across the sleep-softened faces of friends and lovers. She said nothing. She craned her head back and rolled it side to side across the top of the throne's backrest, to carve out a cradle for her skull in the soft-packed sand. At the edges of her vision, the desert blew away, curling in the wind like ocean surf, dissipating into the air. She closed her eyes and slept the dreamless, nourishing, ungrateful sleep of the innocent.

TWENTY HOURS

After I killed my wife, I had twenty hours before her new body finished printing downstairs. I thought about how to spend the time. I could clean the house, as a show of contrition, and when she returned to find me sitting at the shining kitchen island, knickknacks in place on dusted shelves, a pot of soup on the stove, we might not even need to discuss it. I could buy flowers. I could watch the printing, which still fascinated me, the weaving and webbing of each layer of tissue, the cross-sectional view of her internal workings like the ringed sections of a tree trunk.

I had poisoned her, a great wallop of poison in her morning coffee. So I didn't have the defense of passion, a momentary loss of reason. Poison took forethought. Poison said: I wanted to be apart from you for a while. Then why not just leave the house? Why not go for a walk? No, it said more than that. Poison said: I wanted you to not exist for a while. I wanted to move through the world without you in it.

There'd been no choking, gasping, flailing, spewing. Connie simply keeled over at the table. The soft *thunk* of her weighty head, the clatter of her empty cup tipping off the saucer, spilling its dregs. Painless, I hoped, though I would have to take her word for it later, either way. A large dose for a small woman—when she's been driving our car, I'll find the seat raised and pushed as far forward as it goes, so she can reach the pedals and see over the steering wheel. I wrapped her briskly in a sheet, put her out on the porch, and filled out the online form for same-day pickup.

Connie has killed me only once. We'd spent a week car camping in a state park, four hours away, in that last week of the season where the frozen ground sucks heat out through the layers of your tent floor, sleeping pad, and sleeping bag, keeping most people away. She'd done most of the packing, loading the hatchback so full I couldn't see out the back window as I drove. And then one morning, as we packed our day bags for a twenty-mile loop, she informed me she'd borrowed our neighbor Jim's rifle. She'd told him she was afraid of bears. We called Jim an old coot in private, with affection. She slung the rifle over her back and wore it as we set off down the path. I was glad, in a way. I'd been curious about the experience, but whenever I tried to do it myself, I chickened out at the last minute.

She walked in front wherever the path narrowed, leaving me to stare at the long wooden barrel cutting diagonally across her upper back, below her short ponytail. She eventually led me off path, into the woods, and there was something vaguely erotic about it, a tugging. The memory of being a teenager, a girl pulling me by the hand from a bush party, away from the bonfire and into the sultry dark, to become invisible bodies among the trees.

And oh, how Connie looked when she turned to face me, as she shouldered the rifle. How she did not hesitate. Her mouth upturned, her eyes—not hard, just clear, certain, confident. Her cheeks flushed from the cold and the exertion of the hike.

One shot, extremely close range, to the face. I had the sensation of being blown backward. I would later conflate the memory with a chewing gum commercial I'd seen as a kid, where a man gets blown out of his shoes *by flavor*, rocketed out of frame, his empty brown loafers left behind. I was shot out the back of myself like a cannon. Her beloved face, explosive noise, nothingness. I thought, later, that if she'd shot me through the heart or the lungs, or even if she'd beheaded me with an axe, there would have been an in between, a liminal moment where my eyes were still connected to my brain, still sending signals. Time to look at my ruined body, to see her reaction, see us both splattered with gore. My death felt clean to me, precise, surgical, even though I knew, in reality, it had to have been anything but. Like she knew the pinprick-sized location above the stem of my spine, behind the Cupid's bow of my upper lip, in the center of my brain—where my soul resided, and took it out with a perfect bull's-eye shot. That's who she was.

When I woke up on the printer tray at home, I felt no more disoriented than I did in a hotel bed, that moment of dislocation. I padded naked through the house to the master bathroom, showered, dried, dressed. The dark, silent house was what unnerved me. I knew it took twenty hours to reprint me from checkpoint. Had she come home and left on some errand? Had she never come home?

She told me, later, that she made it back to our campsite without encountering anyone, wiped herself down as best she could, changed into fresh clothes. She packed up and drove our car to a motel at the next exit. It was alpine-lodge themed, painted wood with whimsical cutouts and spade-topped fencing that might once have been charming but now had that eerie blend of the childish and the decaying. As she requested a room, she noticed a small streak of blood on her neck in the mirror behind the front desk.

That evening, her hair still dripping wet from the shower, she went down to the attached bar. The place was packed, the tight spaces between tables made tighter by bulky winter coats slung over chairbacks and muddy slush dragged in on boots. She took a seat at the bar that wasn't really a seat, a barstool wedged in a corner made by the path to the kitchen. Hockey blared on the TV. The bartender threw down a coaster in front of my wife and tilted her head without speaking. My wife got a rye and Coke, not usually her drink. They served food, and she hadn't eaten since before the long hike, so she ordered the meatloaf. (You hate meatloaf, I said, as she recounted the story. She shrugged. It had been so long since she'd had meatloaf, she explained, she couldn't remember if she actually disliked it or if that was just something she said.)

Strangers bumped her elbows. A man leaned over her shoulder to order at the bar, pushing his pelvis up against the back of her stool, his cheek nearly brushing hers. She was staring up at the TV, leaning her head on her right fist, tiny figures whipping across a white background, the announcer at breathless auctioneer speed. Her left hand curled loosely around her drink. The man tapped her wedding ring with his index finger. Where's your husband, he asked. A flirtatious twinkle.

I, she started. And then she laughed. Not her usual laugh but a madwoman's laugh, shrill and hysterical. I'm a widow, I guess. Technically. She laughed more, and the man looked spooked. He took his drink and backed away.

Or so she says. Maybe they went back to her room together. What right would I have to complain? I was dead.

The printer is outrageously expensive, both the initial cost and the upkeep—the data storage, connectivity service, matter re-fill tanks, registration with law enforcement and local hospitals. Most people associate the printers with the monstrously wealthy, something one acquires along with a superyacht, a private jet, a staffed mansion. When they first came out, it didn't feel surprising that these people would be shielded from certain kinds of death.

My wife and I are that other kind of rich: the misers among you, in our quaint three-bedroom house in the suburbs, un renovated since the 1990s, one modest hatchback car between us, our big-box store generic clothes, our outdated phones and computers. Lucky in our birthright privileges, in our inheritance, in our jobs, in the stock market, hoarding cash for reasons that stopped being clear to us long ago, that make less and less sense the older we get. We have no children. Our parents are dead. We keep working, we clean our own toilets, rake our own yard. We use our vacations to go camping in-state. We'll give it all away upon our deaths, and there will be one of those shocked news stories about people like us and our secret millions, the sudden windfall upon our pet causes and distant nieces and nephews. Why don't we help anyone while we're alive? Our once-reasonable anxieties grown distorted, outsized, habitual. There will never be enough money to make us feel safe.

So you can see how the printer became the one frivolity to seduce us. We'd leaned in together over my wife's laptop at the kitchen table, scrolling through the sales pitch. You embedded a device under the skin of your thigh that performed a full-body scan, drawing up specs for a printed copy of your body. The device re-scanned every ten seconds, noting changes and rewriting the data from your last checkpoint accordingly. The specs for your next printed body changed with you, ten seconds at a time. When you died, your consciousness would be uploaded at the moment of death. A body would be printed based on the most recent checkpoint with complete, coherent, functional data—the most recent version of your body that wasn't already dying.

But the longer the gap between that checkpoint and the moment of death, the more likely it was that the new body would reject the consciousness. It wouldn't take, the mind would dissipate, and you would be truly dead. Consciousnesses were too large to be stored for long, only immediately transferred, and the compatibility window was a matter of minutes. So you couldn't keep downloading to a young, unblemished body. The printer couldn't save you from cancer, or heart disease, or aging, or even a slow, festering wound. It didn't make you immortal. It didn't protect you from the ways most of us go, only from a slim category of quick, unlikely deaths. Accidental death upon impact, an air conditioner to the head, a sixteen-wheeler at highway speed. Swift, cold-blooded acts of violence.

Once we'd had it for a few years, the elaborate machinery in the basement, the plastic pellets in our legs, this money pit draining down our accounts like nothing we'd ever done or owned in our lives, it started to feel ridiculous. Such wildly expensive insurance against the improbable. And then—like most users, I imagine; the parties of the ultrarich must be bloodbaths—we felt tempted. Curious.

I've killed her several times. She's killed herself a couple more. She says it's the same for her as it was for me, less than a blip, a simultaneous exit and entrance, awake on the tray. No ghostly attachment to or sentiment for the old body, wherever it was abandoned. I like to think mine made a fine dinner for wolves, ravens, maggots—was immediately useful in a way I sometimes doubt I have ever been. But I sometimes wonder if Connie is lying, if she goes somewhere else, if she experiences something profound, or comforting, or beautiful. If she brings something back with her. Otherwise, I can't understand why she's done it more than once. There's always a risk she'll take a little too long to die, that there'll be two bodies and no Connie in this world in the end.

If I was planning to clean the house and buy flowers while she was gone, I had lots of time. I'd killed her on a Sunday morning. I went to carry some dishes that I'd left in the living room to the kitchen sink, but I ended up settling into the couch, turning on the TV. Sinking in. I fell asleep for about an hour. Still plenty of time.

Our neighbor on the other side, not Jim, once confessed to me about having an affair. Darren and I talk over the fence when we both happen to be outside, sitting on our back decks, avoiding yard work, tending to meat on the grill. Or he waves me over when I'm shoveling snow, washing the car, taking out the trash, and we stand in his driveway and chat. I don't think we've ever intentionally made plans to spend time together.

It started out as a lark, he said. Download the app, make a fake profile, see what was out there. After a while, he started using a real photo of himself, with a fake name and a lowered age. Just a game, confined to the imaginary realm of his phone, to feel a little better about himself. Hard boundaries he told himself he'd never cross, until he did. Messaging women just to see if he could get a response. A flirtatious back-and-forth with one woman. Texting her from his actual phone number. Photos. A phone call. More phone calls, in his parked car at the gas station, in the bathroom at work. How every step seemed defensible, every escalation minor. How he would message this other woman after fights with his wife, when she shuddered away from his touch in her sleep, when she *tsk*ed and took their crying toddler out of his arms, as though she knew better what to do. How at first, he even convinced himself it made him a better husband and father, having this outlet.

Poison was like that. An intrusive thought, sated by an internet search, like so many other idle curiosities. Researching dosage and, most importantly, speed. Advice on a forum that led to another forum that led to a non-indexed website. Just looking. Just reading. Another day, I started to enter my information, but didn't click "submit"—this happened several times. I often dither over online purchases this way. And then one day, I followed through. I made the order.

Nearly two months later, when I'd almost forgotten about it, a padded envelope arrived in the mail, seemingly full of small junk products—hair rollers, key chains, pads of Post-it Notes, toothbrushes. Jumbled among them, in the center, was a two-inch plastic baggie of what looked like crystalized sugar.

I meant just to keep it, just to have it, to know that it was there, tucked into a balled-up pair of socks in our dresser. When I made Connie coffee in the morning before she was awake, when I poured red wine in the kitchen while she was in the living room, I found myself lingering, staring into the dusky, opaque liquids that could conceal and dissolve. Like Darren's photos of another woman's body, her whispered flattery in the dark, it was an escape hatch, a door to the world without our wives, to our larger selves beyond them, to what might still be possible.

I never meant to use it.

And then I never meant to use it again.

I got breakfast from the McDonald's drive-through and brought it home. Connie thought McDonald's was disgusting. With the sandwich wrapper still in front of me on my desk, blotched by congealing American cheese, I opened a porn site without headphones, but this quickly felt petty and juvenile. I felt tethered to the house, knowing Connie was being rebuilt downstairs, her mind injected into each extruded cell. Even though she hadn't felt the same way when she'd killed me. She'd let me wake up on the printer tray alone while she stared up at the water-damaged ceiling of a motel room, a long curl of paint splitting away from its home.

A vertical banner advertised a cam girl site. I clicked through, something I'd never done. Enter your credit card info for access, but it wouldn't be charged right away, you could sit in on any girl's public stream for free. You paid only to give her gifts, make requests, see her in private rooms. To get her attention.

Typing in the numbers felt genuinely transgressive. Maybe that's pathetic. Most of the public options were women posing and chatting in lingerie—I gathered you had to pay for nudity and sex acts—but the one I lingered on was the most clothed, in a short floral dress and knee socks. She sat with her legs tucked under her, feet to the side. She had gangly proportions, a long, narrow face with a long, narrow nose, further elongated by long, dead-straight hair. A long, narrow torso, extravagantly long, thin limbs, small breasts. Pale with dark, vampiric makeup. Her age was inscrutable, the girlish outfit paradoxically aging her. Backgrounded by a pinned-up bed-sheet. A ring light reflected in her eyes, as well as the changing flicker and scroll of her laptop as she read the chat and cooed her responses. I felt the presence of the chat in the room with me, some five hundred—five hundred! A Broadway theater audience, hunched and breathing together. Only a small minority were typing, making the same demands over and over, the same compliments, what they would do to her. Show us, show me. We love you, I love you, I want to destroy you. She'd be going into her paid room soon, and didn't we want to come?

Connie in the basement, half-built. Connie in the motel bar. I typed: *my wife died.* It joined the fast-moving, garishly colored river of text. Because I'd never spent any money, my username and text were a muted, hard-to-read gray, while big spenders were in flashy fonts, their names decorated with little icons of flair. And then, after ten seconds of lag, our hostess read my words aloud: My wife died. Oh, eggmcmuffin2026, I'm so sorry, she said. I hope you'll come along to my private room and I can help make you feel better.

I felt a wild jolt. She'd noticed me! Grayed-out, invisible me. She said my name! She said it smoothly, warmly, without irony, like eggmcmuffin2026 was my real name, like it was her secret, private name just for me. Like I was special, picked from obscurity out of a crowd.

I closed the browser window. It was past noon now, and for the ten steps from the side door to the car when I'd gone to McDonald's, I could tell it was going to be a beautiful autumn day, cold and crisp, the full splendor of sun. But the study where I sat, the heavy curtains drawn, felt subterranean and dank, reeking of hash browns and burned coffee and my unshowered flesh. Clean the house, I thought again. Buy flowers. Make soup.

I woke up on the couch a second time, to the sounds of footsteps on our front porch. It was dark outside. I peered out the narrow window by the front door and saw two men in white jumpsuits and masks lifting Connie's last printed body. They nodded to me before carrying her to their truck. I wondered, briefly, if Connie would be upset about the lost bedsheet.

In the kitchen, I pulled out a couple of frozen pork ribs and all the wilted vegetables that could go in a simple soup. The oven clock read six o'clock. I chopped one onion before I felt too hungry to continue.

I ordered takeout from our favorite Thai restaurant. There was a florist on the same block. We always drove there, even though it was less than two miles away. We'd get into the car on autopilot, pull out from the driveway, and then one of us would announce, We should walk next time.

I was still in my pajamas—I'd worn them in the McDonald's drive-through line—and still hadn't done the laundry. I put on a pair of gray sweatpants and threw on the windbreaker hanging by the door, also gray, with a red chevron pattern across the collar.

The walk took longer than I expected. Cars rumbled close on stretches without sidewalk or shoulder, unlit roads bounded by brush where I stumbled on loose gravel in the dark. The cold cut straight through my jacket and ratty sleep shirt. When I finally reached the short commercial strip, the Thai restaurant lit up in the middle like a beacon, my nose was running and my hands stung.

I stopped before the plate glass window at the front of the restaurant. The light of its awning reflected strangely on the surface, such that I could see inside, but parts of my reflection were superimposed on top. Faint, ghostly shapes haunted tables of oblivious diners. My face was only a smudge, my clothes more distinct, particularly the white drawstring of my pants and red blocks of color in the jacket. I felt a wave of déjà vu, the sense that I recognized the fragmented person in the window, but not as myself.

I looked down at my frozen hands, blooming pink and white. My printed hands. For the first time in a long while, I thought about how these were not the hands my mother held when I was born, not the hands I blistered and covered in ink when I was in school, the hands Connie held at the altar. But that was true of everyone. Skin cells replace themselves every few weeks, bone and fat every ten years. Like the Ship of Theseus, an enigma I'd first heard as a child: If you replaced every plank and component of a ship over time, until nothing of the original remained, was it the same ship? The printer was only a difference of speed. If a machine faithfully re-created you at the cellular level, particle by particle, the enamel of your teeth and the lenses of your eyes and each remaining ovum and all your flaws and all the ways you dis-appoint yourself and the ones you love, was that you, or someone new? Where was Connie right now, bundled on a disposal truck or in our basement or in the ether of space?

And then I realized whom I saw in the window. My first job, in high school, had been at a video-rental place. A guy would come in, always with a wave of people so we might not notice him, or late on weeknights when I was working alone, knowing I'd be too scared to approach him and kick him out. He would find the spot in the store he wanted, the movie box he wanted—a woman laughing on the cover of a rom-com or mid-shriek on a horror film, a headless torso or disembodied ass on a raunchy comedy—and start masturbating. My older coworkers told me that every video store had at least one of these guys. We called the cops on him a couple of times, but he fled before they arrived, and even though we had him on our security cameras, they said there was nothing they could do. When I was alone with him in the store, I strained not to look in his direction, as though by not looking, I could will him out of existence, to the point where I would have had trouble recognizing his face. If he were in a different set of clothes, I could have passed him on the street without knowing. I knew the back of his head. I knew what he wore to the store, because it was always the same: loose, gray, drawstring sweatpants and a gray windbreaker with red at the collar.

I suddenly didn't want to go inside, didn't want to disturb the dinners of these other people, talking and laughing and eating intently, each table lit by its own hanging fixture like the bounds of a theater stage, a tableau of their lives. I remembered sitting across from Connie at a table in the back as she said that she liked going out to eat because it was the only time she had my full attention. At the time, I'd taken it as a complaint about how often we ate in front of the TV, how I mindlessly reached for my phone while she was talking. That she was calling me generally inattentive, unloving. As I stood on the sidewalk—the couple at the table against the window now aware of my looming presence, pausing their conversation to glance in my direction—the meaning shifted, became a declaration of how desperately she wanted my full attention, how much she loved me.

The florist was closed.

On the walk home, the heat fading from my bagged, boxed noodles, the streets were darker still, house lights extinguished. Over a guardrail, I could see down a steep ramble of wild blackberry bushes, where we could go picking next summer. I passed a drive-up espresso shack with a marquee that read *new! salted caramel hazelnut triple fudge brownie mocha* and could picture Connie wrinkling her nose in distaste. The gibbous moon was hazed over, a thin, mournful cloud layer. She wouldn't see this moon, this night.

Once, I hit Connie across the back of her head with a baseball bat. That was a mistake. She was standing in our backyard, alone, staring up at the stars. From the way she held her hand, I knew she was craving a cigarette; she'd quit a decade ago. She didn't turn as I strode up behind her and swung. She went down, and I was so afraid that she wasn't dead, that she wouldn't die quickly enough, that she wouldn't come back. So I had to hit her again and again, had to turn her to pulp, as fast as possible, sobbing, my whole body awash with terror, blood spreading through the soil and the grass.

When she sat up from the printer tray that time, I was sitting beside it. I leapt to embrace her. She didn't ask why I'd done it. Didn't ask if it was because she told the same stories over and over from the same small window of her life, a time before me. Didn't ask if it was because of the way she sighed when I had to ask where we kept the lightbulbs. Didn't ask if it was because I would never again sit up all night talking to a romantically interesting stranger. Didn't ask if it was because I increasingly looked into her face and saw my own face, an uncanny familial drift, the fat settling in the same places, because we were aging into the same person, the product of consuming the same things and being exposed to the same things and infecting each other.

It's a farcically old-fashioned, misogynistic joke: Take my wife, please. I could imagine the horror on even Darren's face, who could never dream of affording a printer, who was scarcely aware of their existence. You want to kill your wife? Then get divorced. You don't even have kids! But it's the opposite: I want her to come back. I want to sit shivering on the cold concrete floor of our unfinished basement, the washing machine against my back, a widowed wreck, boredom and disdain and resentment drained away as after a medieval bloodletting, knowing who I'd be without her, full of new things to tell her, knowing she's the only person who will understand. She didn't have to ask why I'd done it.

I ran out of time. I abandoned the soup midway, once night rolled into morning, and it felt like it made more sense to make her pancakes instead. The kitchen was a disaster. I started the laundry but got only as far as loading the clean clothes into the dryer.

Connie appeared at the top of the stairs in a rumpled set of pajamas she'd pulled out, holding the laundry basket against her hip. She sat at the kitchen island. I put down a plate of pancakes and bacon in front of her. I put on some music. She smiled faintly, a mysterious smile, gone and back from somewhere I could never truly know, all her secrets her own, fascinating again.

THE DOLL

My mother was the one who found Mr. Mullen. She was an early riser, chased out of sleep by her task list for the day. She looked out the window over our kitchen sink and into the Mullens' carport. Though the Mullens kept it very neat, my mother had always found the carport obscene, sitting exposed among our garages, our sleeping cars and little-used power tools kept hidden and out of sight as God intended. Mr. Mullen hung from the central beam.

The rest of us lived in two-story homes that crowded to the lots' edges, hipped roofs matching the cube-like dimensions as neatly as a lid to a jar, our driveways and yards stout and begrudging. The Mullens' house, conversely, was a midcentury bungalow with a long, low roofline, orange-toned brick and wood, with that carport and a sprawling, unruly backyard—the specific architectural dream of a designer or previous owner, representing a specific moment in time. Our houses were specifically for the dreamless, signifying nothing.

If it had been one of the other parents, they might have called the police first. My mother sprinted out of the house and across the street. Knowing my mother, she wasn't thinking about saving him. She would've seen that it was too late while she was jogging down our driveway and up his, or even from our kitchen—how he had become one stiff, contiguous object, tapering down to his feet, his hands a purplish blue.

Knowing my mother, she was rushing to prevent anyone else from seeing him. She would've been appalled at the self-ishness of hanging himself in the open carport, exposed to any passerby. To us, the neighborhood children. She climbed onto the stepladder he'd used and cut him down with his pruning shears, and he dropped hard to the concrete floor. She took a drop sheet off some paint cans and threw it over him before she called 911. The rest of the street woke to the sirens.

The Mullens had rented a lake house for the first week of summer vacation, with a gas heater that had been dormant through the off-season. Mrs. Mullen and the three Mullen children had gone ahead on Wednesday morning. When he joined them on Friday night, his wife and children were all lifeless in their beds. It was later determined to be carbon monoxide poisoning.

In Connor Feldspar's front yard, sharing a bag of licorice ropes, we talked it through. Mr. Mullen arrives at the lake house, finds it dark, the porch light off. He's surprised that no one is waiting up for him. He opens the screen door quietly, not wanting to wake the youngest Mullen, just eighteen months old. He goes into the dark master bedroom, climbs into bed with his wife, tries to wake her with an embrace.

I was one kind of ghoul: a boy to whom nothing bad had happened, all suffering unreal as comic book gore. Connor was another: a child to whom many bad things had happened, who relished any story where he was not the victim. Connor and I weren't friends at school, but the neighborhood yards in the summertime were a different, neutral place, full of unlikely alliances.

Olivia Meier sat between us and listened intently. She was the youngest of us, a rodent-faced girl with beady eyes and a habit of chewing on her fists. The dead baby fascinated her, blending in her mind with the cherubs painted on our Sunday school wall. She imagined little Jordie Mullen sprouting angel wings and a full head of golden ringlets, his baby blanket twisted modestly around his waist, a playful smile on his lipstick-red mouth.

Isaac and Abby Gibbs, enemies the other nine months of the year, finished each other's sentences in the summer. They wondered aloud about the last night the whole Mullen family was alive. Their last meal. Something easy to make in an unfamiliar kitchen, ready-made vacation food, canned ravioli or frozen dinners. Mrs. Mullen puts the baby to bed, tells the two older kids—brother and sister, like Isaac and Abby—to settle down, stop horsing around on the rented bunk bed and its creaky wooden ladder. She tucks them in. She turns off the light, shaking her head as the whispers and giggles start up again before she's even shut the door. What did the Mullen kids talk about, not knowing it was their last conversation? When they fell asleep, did they dream? What happens in a dream interrupted by death?

Connor and I drew the conversation back to the bodies. I'd read that people who die of carbon monoxide poisoning sometimes look healthy and alive, a rosy pink glow to their skin, because the end product of the gas turns blood vessels cherry red. Like Olivia, I pictured Mrs. Mullen and the kids as angelic, more beautiful in death than they were in life, their faces set forever in soft expressions of sleep. Connor saw them like molted snakeskins, a remnant left for Mr. Mullen. Like a farewell note on the kitchen counter: Gone on ahead, see you soon.

The story occupied us all summer. The adults said *how terrifying, what a tragedy, could have happened to anyone*, their fear so false it sounded smug. Because it hadn't happened to anyone. It had happened to the Mullens.

Caitlin and Gordon Mullen had gone to a private progressive school that started a half hour earlier than our public school. We'd seen them being driven by Mrs. Mullen in their wood-paneled station wagon while the rest of us waited at the corner for the yellow school bus. They studiously didn't look back at us, their bowl-cut blond heads facing forward, squished together in the back beside the baby's car seat.

About a year before they died, my mother had invited Mrs. Mullen and Gordon over on a Saturday—Gordon to play with me, and Mrs. Mullen to take tea in the kitchen with my mother. Caitlin and Mrs. Mullen showed up instead. Caitlin wore white knee socks and a long-sleeved dress, her hair pinned to one side with a barrette. All the other neighborhood girls dressed in jeans and corduroys. The boys wore oversized basketball shorts as deep into the winter as possible, as though we might be called up by the NBA at any moment.

"Oh," my mother said, taking in the two Mullens on her doorstep.

"Gordon had a piano lesson," Mrs. Mullen said.

"Oh," she repeated, the syllable rich with meaning. To me, she said, "Matt, why don't you take Caitlin to play in the living room?"

I usually took my playmates to my bedroom. "My toys and stuff are all upstairs," I said.

She clenched her face into a smile. "Then go choose the ones you want and bring them down."

Caitlin followed me up the stairs. We walked with a slow, odd decorum. I had friends who were girls, but Caitlin made me uneasy, her girlishness turned up alien-high. I showed her my comic books, my figurines, my model cars, my bin of Lego. "What do you want to play?" I asked.

"You pick," she said.

"Let's bring the Lego down," I said. The storage tub was so large that I could fit inside and pretend to be bathing in the plastic bricks. I could pull it off the low shelf and onto the floor to play, but it quickly became apparent that it was too heavy for me to get it down the stairs on my own.

"We can carry it together," Caitlin said. We each took a handle. Caitlin, who'd been closer to the stairs, walked backward, and I followed facing forward, the bin between us.

My socked foot slipped at the edge of the carpeted stairs. Righting my footing, I lost my grip on the handle. I grasped at the empty air, then instinctively shut my eyes. I forced myself to open them again. In that one instant, I'd missed Caitlin and the plastic tub tumbling down the stairs, the lid popping off. She was already at the bottom, on her butt, looking beached and bewildered in the flood of multicolored plastic.

Our mothers rushed to the sound of the crash. My mother reached Caitlin first, with a little cry. "What happened?" Mrs.

Mullen looked up at me, still near the top of the stairs, my hands still extended as if to catch something.

My mother knelt beside Caitlin and examined a hole ripped in one of her socks, the scraped knee above it. "I'm fine," Caitlin said. "It's fine."

"I'm sorry," I said, at last. "I slipped."

"Go get the first aid kit," my mother said. I ran to the bathroom, relieved to have a task.

As my mother—and not Mrs. Mullen, strangely—tended to Caitlin's knee, rubbing ointment into the raw scratches, Caitlin repeated, "I'm fine, really. It doesn't hurt."

My mother patted her lightly on the knee, smoothing the bandage. "There you go." She turned back to me and gestured at the spilled Lego. "Matt, clean this up."

"I'll help," Caitlin said.

"No," my mother said. "Matt can do it." She turned to Caitlin's mom. "I'm so sorry about this."

"It's fine," she said. She sounded just like Caitlin, such that her adult voice seemed oddly high and thin, and Caitlin's child voice seemed deep and serious, a compromise between registers. "Really, it's fine."

Caitlin and Mrs. Mullen hovered as I scooped armfuls of Lego back into the bin. "Perhaps," said my mother, "we should try this again some other time."

We didn't. Though my mother was angry with me, when she told my father the story later, it was clear that she blamed the Mullens somehow. "That girl could have broken her neck," she said. "And then where would we be?" She tried to convey all the details of their visit at the same time, out of order, the causality of the fall lost somewhere in the middle. "She was wearing Mary Janes and a dress for a playdate. Can you imagine?"

I know I remember this incident only because Caitlin died, and remembering her as strange, as marked, makes that easier to understand. In our neighborhood, in the absence of real difference, we seized on the minute, the unnameable, the imaginary. I can only imagine what we would have done if we didn't have the Mullens.

Eventually, after we had gone over every aspect of the Mullens' deaths, Connor dared us to go over to their house. It was August by then, and the police tape had been cleared or had blown away, disintegrated in the sun. A lurid stain remained on the floor of the carport. An unfamiliar sedan had been seen parked in the Mullens' driveway; a woman in a cream pantsuit had stepped out, gone inside with a key, come back out, relocked the door, and driven away. She was assumed to be a relative, but not the kind of relative who would get on her hands and knees to take a sponge to the darkened concrete.

The Mullens had a corner lot. It was simple to hop the fence between their backyard and the quiet street, taking turns scrambling over and watching out for cars and adults. We boosted little Olivia over first.

From where we gathered again on the other side, the ambient sound of summer insects seemed heightened, louder than Connor panting to catch his breath. The weeds along the three-sided fence had spread inward and upward: dandelions and tall grasses starting to seed, scalloped and jagged broadleafs that looked like they belonged on a jungle floor. A bush of nettles and trumpet-shaped purple flowers towered regally over the rest. We gravitated toward the toys scattered in the singed grass near the back door, moving as a group.

An underinflated soccer ball yielded to my poking finger. "Don't *touch* anything," Abby hissed. I examined some glass jam jars lined up on a low table of planks hammered together. Each jar had a few inches of potting soil and a shriveled plant inside. A blue plastic watering can was tucked neatly underneath the table. Everything was clearly kid-sized, with the air of one of our own experiments.

I joined Olivia and Isaac beside a toy stroller, two hammocks of pink fabric in a pink plastic frame, a baby doll nestled inside. It was turned onto its side, the arms and legs drawn up, a realistic sleeping pose despite the forever-open acrylic eyes. The doll's felt pajamas had been bleached by the sun, the pink stripes faded to nearly the same shade as the white ones. The fingers and feet were molded in a curled shape, loose fists and tucked-under toes.

Olivia crouched to examine the doll. Abby hissed at her as well, from where she'd been trying to peer into the only unshaded back window.

"That thing is creepy as hell," Isaac said.

"I have the same one," Olivia said.

A chill passed through us.

"Okay, it's time to go," Isaac announced. Jokey, mock-frightened.

Connor sidled up next to me as we started back toward the fence. "Hey, Matt. I dare you to take the doll."

We stopped and looked back at the doll. The sunlight reflected off the pink nightcap and gown, making the doll seem as though it had a faint internal glow, a blush upon its plastic cheeks. "Why would I want a doll?" I said.

"Are you scared of it?"

"No, I just don't want it."

"Because you're scared."

"What do I tell my mom? Where am I supposed to say it came from?"

"You don't hide stuff from your mom? You tell your mom everything?"

"Oh, shut up," Abby said. She grabbed the doll and tucked it under her arm like a football. "There, I have the doll. Who cares. Let's go."

Abby crept into Isaac's room the next morning. She tucked the baby doll into the bed beside him. He woke up with its shining eyes peering into his own. As he started to scream, Abby tackled him, covering his mouth and throwing the doll under the bed just as their father came in. Abby recounted this as she presented the doll back to us, where we had convened once more in the strip of grass bordering the concrete pad that took up most of Connor's backyard. "Isaac doesn't want it in the house anymore," she said. Isaac sat cross-legged just behind her, looking down into the triangle between his legs.

"I dreamt about them," he said.

"The Mullens?" I said.

He nodded. When he didn't elaborate, Abby spoke for him. "He dreamt that Gordon was in his room. Wearing his clothes."

"My basketball uniform," Isaac clarified.

"Then he sat down at the desk and started doing one of Isaac's summer reading assignments."

"Sounds great," Connor said. "I wish Gordon's ghost would do *my* homework."

"Then you take it," Abby said, thrusting the doll at him.

Connor leaned back. "Gross. No way."

"Who's scared now?" I said.

Connor flushed. "Fine. I don't care. I'll give it to Albie to chew on." He gestured over his shoulder, where Albie, the Feldspars' nasty little terrier mix, yipped and banged at the sliding glass door.

"No!" Olivia cried. "Don't do that. She's probably lonely. I'll take her. She can hang out with my dolls." Connor didn't disguise his relief.

When Olivia returned to Connor's the next day, she was holding the doll upside down by the ankle, the long pink nightcap dragging on the ground. "Albie can have her," she said.

"What did she do?" Abby asked.

"She switched places with my doll."

"What do you mean?"

"My doll, that's the same as her—her name is Bebe. I sleep with her. I put Caitlin's doll on the shelf with the other dolls and stuffies. But I woke up and Bebe was on the shelf and *she* was in my bed." Olivia flipped the doll right side up as she shoved it in our faces for emphasis, holding it under the arms like it was a real baby.

"She did the same thing to me," Isaac said.

"No, that was me," Abby reminded him. "I put her in your bed. It was a joke."

"Are you sure you're not just confusing them?" I said. "If she and Bebe look alike?"

"I would *never* mix them up." Olivia stomped her foot, indignant. "Bebe's nightgown is all pink. This one has stripes. Plus Bebe is newer. This one is all faded and icky." She shook the doll and something rattled inside. "Somebody get rid of her. She tried to replace Bebe!"

"Okay, okay," Connor said, taking the doll. He went to the door, slid it open, and called for Albie. As the dog bounded from somewhere deeper in the house, the rest of us shrank back. At one time or another, Albie had nipped at all of our ankles and probing fingers. His razor teeth seemed too large for his tiny head, which was no bigger than a baseball.

Standing at the threshold, Connor offered Albie the doll in a singsong voice. "Here you go, boy. I've got a new chewie for you."

Albie sniffed the doll's chest. He looked up at Connor suspiciously, then slowly backed up, returning to the shadowy house, where he growled and resumed his shrill barking.

"Come on," Connor said, thrusting the doll at Albie, who jumped away from it, still yipping. "Just take it."

"He knows it's haunted," Isaac said. Olivia nodded.

"This stupid dog never trusts me," Connor said. "Albie, don't be a dick. Take the toy. Take the—ow!" Albie had nipped at Connor's wrist. Connor flung the doll through the door. Albie leapt away before it could strike him. He stood over the prone form, barking into its blank, contented face.

I was the first to arrive at Connor's the next day. He grimly ushered me through the front hall and the kitchen, out the back door, as usual. He stopped at the edge of the concrete pad, gesturing into the narrow yard.

The baby doll's head poked up from a pile of dirt, freshly torn out of the sod. The sleepy expression, rosebud lips molded into a pout, was made more unnerving by the mud streaked across the pink nightcap and open eyes.

"Did Albie bury it or did you?" I asked.

Connor glared at me. "Why would *I* do that?"

"I don't know. To freak me out?"

"Well, I didn't."

"Did you have a nightmare too?"

Connor's face purpled. He walked over and yanked the doll forcefully out of the ground by the nightcap, like pulling up a carrot. "You have to take it," he said. The doll swung back and forth in his grip, the motion nauseating.

"I don't want it," I said.

"You're the only one who hasn't had it in your house."

"So?"

"So it's *your turn*."

"But now it's all dirty."

Connor flung the doll in frustration, just as he had the day before. It landed at my feet facing up, staring at the blue of the sky, still curling its plastic fists.

I carried the doll home in a plastic grocery bag from Connor's kitchen. I tied the handles together and then quickly untied them, feeling like I was suffocating her. I didn't want it in my room, but I couldn't think of anywhere else it wouldn't be discovered by my parents, so I tucked it into the back of my closet.

I positioned her sitting up, her back against the wall, her head sticking out of the bag. She slumped forward, the top of the nightcap drooping over her face. She looked defeated.

"Sorry," I said, covering her with a box of my winter clothes.

While my mother carried dinner from the kitchen to the dining room, my parents talked about the Mullens' house like I wasn't there. "It's going to be demolished," my mother said.

"Where did you hear that?"

She ignored my father's question. "His sister sold to a developer. They're going to build a house with more livable square footage on the footprint, more in keeping with the neighborhood."

"Who told you that?" he asked again.

"I read the sign out front."

"What sign?"

"The piece of paper on the front door."

My father thought this through. "You mean you looked up the construction permits?"

"Of course." She set down the potatoes and joined us at the table. "That's why it's there. For concerned neighbors. You know it only had one bathroom? A family of five, that big corner lot, one bathroom."

My father had been studying her. I tried to see what he saw. Her slim hips and arms, her small, pointed features. She was wearing cropped turquoise pants, a matching turquoise scarf holding her hair back from her face, her morning makeup still brightening her eyes at the end of the day. She did not look like someone who could cut down a corpse with garden shears.

She started making up a plate for me. Her eyes on the Salisbury steak, she continued, "It'll be loud, but I'm looking forward to it being gone. Bring the bulldozers, I say."

"I never understood what you had against that house," my father said. "It's historic. Not from the most picturesque decade, but historic nonetheless." My mother paused meaningfully, holding a scoop of steamed broccoli aloft. "I mean, what you had against the house *before*," he added.

"It was poorly maintained. The property was messy, an eyesore." She passed me my plate and started filling another for my father. "'Historic' was never the word that came to mind."

"I thought the mess looked . . . intentional. Bohemian, maybe."

She tilted the full plate of food toward him, like she wanted him to see it but might not give it to him, a hostage. "The Mullens were a husband and wife like any other around here," she said. "Three kids. A new baby. A mortgage. There wasn't anything bohemian about them." Checking herself, she added quickly, "It's a terrible, terrible tragedy."

"He must have loved them a lot," my father mused.

"He found his whole family dead. Who could recover from that? Who wouldn't do what he did?"

My father reached for his dinner, so my mother had to pass it to him. As he started cutting into his steak patty, she watched with pursed lips, not assembling her own plate. Life without us, my father's silence seemed to say, would not be mortally unbearable. Perhaps he even cultivated a fantasy of it—a blameless, sympathetic escape from all that bound him here. He chewed the soft, re-formed meat.

After dinner and my bath, after my parents said good night and I was alone in bed, the doll had a palpable presence in the room. I thought, again, about the gas leak that killed the Mullens. How trustfully we went to sleep each night, certain we'd rise the next day, everything and everyone where we left it. We'd heard over and over that the gas was colorless and odorless, but I pictured it as a low-lying blue fog, the color of cigarette smoke or the last light of day.

I saw it seeping into their cabin through a door left slightly ajar, winding through the crack like jet stream over the wing of an airplane. Bounded loosely like a ghost, it traveled from room to room, finding each member of the family. It settled over the Mullens' sleeping faces, getting sucked into their nostrils in thin runnels. Divided in substance and united in purpose like an army of insects, crawling into their soft tissues and orifices.

The gas might have been in my room right then, rolling over the lip of the window that had been left open to the late summer heat, entering me with every breath I took. I pulled the blanket over my head. My breathing had become fast and shallow, making me feel light-headed—or was that an effect of the gas?

The blue cloud grew squiggly, amorphous limbs that ended in smaller appendages, akin to fingers. It wandered through our house, tracing the photos on my parents' bedroom wall, me as a fat-faced baby in the bathtub alongside a photo of them, much younger, standing on the stern of a boat. I'd never asked where that photo was taken, what marina and body of water shone in the background, why they were there, what sun could tan them so darkly and make them laugh so freely.

The fog-fingers reached the head of my parents' bed. They inserted themselves into my mother's mouth and up her nose, making her mind swim as the tissue of her brain softened. The gas liquefied her brain until it poured out her ears, onto the pillow, like a viscous gray paint. She and I drowned in dreams, becoming sleepy-eyed, pink-cheeked baby dolls. Posable and firm as plastic.

The fog then whispered to my father, sounding like his own voice, speaking to himself. It lifted him from the bed and onto his feet, wobbly and unbalanced—a flat-footed wooden nutcracker. The fog dressed him, wrapping a button-down shirt around his stiff wooden shoulders like a shawl, and put a suitcase in his hand. It blew open the front door with the force of a windstorm, pulled the sun up from behind the horizon like a stage prop on a string. My doll-father wandered out, blinking awake, down our driveway and down our street and down an endless, open road beyond, two rows of smiling, levered teeth painted on his face.

"So we agree," Abby said, "that the doll is haunted."

Olivia nodded solemnly. The rest of us, the boys, looked away. Though Connor and Isaac were older than Abby, she was the tallest, and it gave her an air of authority. Even then, we knew it wouldn't last much longer. We'd noted the omen of Isaac's large feet and hands, his limbs stretching like putty.

We sat in a circle with the doll at the center, still inside the grocery bag with the sides folded down, like the doll was emerging from a plastic cocoon. "What do we do with it?" I asked.

"You're not leaving it here," Connor said.

"I'm not taking it."

"Me neither."

"Us neither."

"Let's put it back," Isaac said.

"We can't."

"Why not?"

"It's a construction site now." I'd woken that morning to the beeping of a bulldozer backing up, the yellow beast taller than the Mullens' fence. "They're going to tear down the house."

"Even better," Connor said. "We can just chuck it over the fence and it'll get buried in the wreckage."

"Let's just throw it away," I said. "In the trash."

Softly, Isaac asked, "Do we really want to make her mad?"

"She'll come back," Olivia said. "If we put her in the trash, she'll come back."

"I like Connor's idea," Abby said. "Maybe she'd like to be buried with her house, and all of Caitlin and Gordon's other toys."

"They don't bury it," I said. "It gets gathered up in a big dumpster bin and taken away. So we might as well put the doll in the trash. She'll go to the same place either way."

"We could bury her ourselves," Abby said.

Olivia shook her head. "She'll come back. The only way to stop her is if we cut her up."

We stared at Olivia. Her knuckles were shiny with saliva, her thin bangs dangling over her brow. "We cut her into pieces, and we each take one," she continued. "We each bury them in a different place, without telling the others where we did it. That way nobody knows where all the pieces are, so she can never get put back together."

Connor broke the long silence that followed. "Jesus Christ, Olivia," he said.

"That's smart," Abby said, thoughtfully.

"Do we have to . . . cut her?" Isaac asked. "The plastic is pretty hard. We'd have to get a saw or something."

"I'm pretty sure we can just take her apart," I said. I grabbed the doll, and everyone reeled slightly back, as they had at the mention of Albie a few days before. I unbuttoned and removed the nightgown. The shirt she wore underneath was sewn onto her torso. I twisted one of her arms, working my fingers into the ball joint, until it popped off. I removed all four of her limbs that way, each one making a satisfying noise as it broke away. Taking her apart was strangely pleasurable, right-feeling, like it was something I was meant to do. As I started twisting and yanking on her head, her face squished under my palm and her limbless torso pressed against my stomach for leverage, I felt my jaw clench, and I became aware of everyone leaning closer to watch. Olivia and Connor looked fascinated, Isaac faintly sick. Abby had a knowing, distant expression that sent a splinter of guilt through me, but somehow also increased the pleasure of distending the doll's face, wringing her neck. It bent time: for a flickering instant, I saw what Abby would look like as an adult, and I saw myself as a grown man. I saw us somewhere together, her staring at me, knowing me, just like this.

The head came off, still wearing its nightcap, its drowsy pout unchanged. Six pieces for five of us—the head, two arms, two legs, and the central torso, neck to crotch. We argued over who would take what. Nobody wanted the head or torso, and everyone wanted the arms. Because I'd risked incurring her wrath by taking her apart, and because Olivia was the youngest, we won. In the end, Abby and Isaac took the head and legs, Connor took the torso, Olivia took the right arm, and I took the left.

Though we agreed never to tell each other where we buried our piece, Connor ended up telling me a few years later. In the rambling, overcrowded junior high we eventually attended, none of us were friends. Connor and I were cut from football tryouts at the same practice, the coach yelling out the numbers pinned to our backs during a drill. Isaac was there too, but he had by then a certain fleet-footed grace, and survived to the next round.

As we waited for our parents to pick us up at the empty school turnabout, Connor confessed he'd gone with his original plan. That night, when the bulldozer was silent, a tarp pinned down by cinder blocks over the partially destroyed house, Connor had thrown the doll's torso over the Mullens' fence, leaving it for the workers to find. He asked what I'd done with her arm, and I went with the most obvious lie—that I'd just buried it in our front yard.

I pictured Olivia, Abby, and Isaac doing the same, finding a spot in their yards where the grass thinned under the myrtle trees, digging down with toy shovels. Or maybe they waited until they were farther from home: Abby packing the head in among their sand toys on a trip to the beach, covering the face in wet sand on a tide flat. Olivia on a hike in the woods, finding a shady spot just off the path, laying a large stone overtop so the plastic fingers couldn't claw their way to freedom.

In truth, I kept the arm. Later still, when I moved away for college, I thought I'd thrown it somewhere in my closet, the closet I hadn't cleaned out as my mother had asked, among toys and papers and barbell weights and clothes for other, discarded visions of myself. But it turned up in the box of books I'd carefully curated to make myself seem smart or cool, to serve as dorm room props, wedged between Hunter S. Thompson and Foucault. The only explanation I could come up with was that it had fallen in, or been placed there in an uncharacteristic prank by my mother. At a Halloween party that year, I put it in the punch bowl, tried to impress girls with its macabre origins. Girls who all, in one way or another, reminded me of Abby or Caitlin. My roommate liked to move the arm around, stick it upright in my shower caddy, throw it into my book bag before I left for class. When I moved to an off-campus apartment with friends, he made sure it went with me, sealed in a box of sweaters. When I moved next, those roommates tossed it in with the pots I'd insisted were mine. I kept thinking I'd lose it, abandon it under a couch between moves, accidentally toss it in a bag for Goodwill, thereby honoring the commitment I'd made. But instead, I kept reaching into a moving box and brushing against the molded hand, the knob I'd torn from its shoulder socket. Maybe the arm will be found among my possessions after I die. It retains the queasy realism of the chubby forearm and plaintive fingers, the same hard sheen on the plastic, never aging.

IN THIS FANTASY

In this fantasy, I'm a landlady in the nineteenth century. A childless spinster, the last of my line, born into wealth, before everything was lost in a generation by my drunkard father. Otherwise penniless at the time of his death, he left me what used to be the city house, the family pied-à-terre: a faded glory, a grand old dame past her prime, like me.

(My fantasies are full of architectural details, window sashes and cornices. The language of home makeover shows, real estate listings, and Regency romance novels.)

I convert it to apartments out of desperation. I have the parlors carved up, section off the bedrooms, pretty up the former maid's quarters, leaving only my childhood bedroom for myself. There I lie on the floor, my ear pressed to a crack between the boards, listening to my first tenants in the room just below. A husband and wife, forever arguing. Cracking and thrashing, muffled shrieks, a thud. A vulgar sort that I wouldn't have associated with in the old days, but these are new days, harder days. The rest of the rooms remain unoccupied.

(In my fantasies, I am always childless, unloved, reclusive—but a landowner.)

One afternoon, the husband away at work, I catch the wife with her lover on the stairwell. Her hand clasps his as she pulls him up toward the rented room. They freeze. I graciously nod and continue down the stairs, as though I've seen nothing. I've come to pity her, to feel she deserves some joy in her life, deserves this surprisingly young man on the stairs, pale and blushing blotchy red, straw-blond hair peeking out from under a newsboy cap. I realize then how young the wife is, how much younger than her husband. She has presumably missed out on making love with someone her own age, just this side of childhood. The discovery and slow unraveling, so unlike the brutality of her husband.

(In this fantasy, I have been celibate for many years, and the longing has died; it's something I remember only abstractly, something for the young. I don't have fantasies where I'm the young, cheating wife, the one rolling over a made bed, drugged light leaking past net curtains, pulled shut in full daylight, where I have the wife's long dark curls, begging to be tugged by the fistful. In my fantasy, I'm graying, powerful, merciful, listening from the room above in judgment like a god.)

The husband picks fights with me. He complains that their room is too cold, the bed sags. He complains there's a draft, so I follow him into their room, the wife out at the market. He can't find it while I'm there. The window fits snugly in its frame, the glass uncracked.

Perhaps, he snarls, your big arse is blocking the breeze.

I nod impassively. Perhaps, I reply.

He complains about the burned toast and weak tea I put out at breakfast, my stinginess with the jam. He imagines me up in my room, right under the eaves where the heat gathers, eating hoarded fresh oranges and fat slabs of buttered bread in bed, and he's not wrong. He blames these inhospitable conditions for his wife's failure to bear children. I don't say: It could be your beatings that prevent the children from taking root. But he can still sense my lack of respect, my lack of deference, unbecoming in a woman, even one my age, even one with the power to throw him and his wife out into the street. He doesn't like it, his inability to dominate me, my frank stare, my seemingly heartless moneygrubbing, the *to let* sign in my own hand, hanging unabashed in the front window.

What kind of woman, he begins, but doesn't know how to finish the question, how to articulate what's wrong with me, why I rile him so.

On another day, as I return from an appointment, I come across the wife in the front sitting room, staring at nothing. I ask if I can get her anything, a cup of tea? She declines the tea, says she would prefer some company instead. We sit together. The silence is awkward. My gaze wanders, and I see the renovation isn't quite what I had hoped, the haste obvious. Everything new looks cheap, and everything old—the windows, the baseboards, the rugs, the ancient wall lamps and chandeliers, the furniture pieces too heavy for my father to lug out and sell—is muted with dust and soot.

Staring into her lap, the wife tells me quietly that she plans to run away with the boy in the cap. I think of myself first—I'm about to lose one of my only sources of revenue, and I will have to find even more tenants. But I also think: Good for her. Out loud, I simply ask when.

Saturday, she says. He goes to the pub after work on Saturdays.

So soon, I say.

I wanted to warn you. Because he'll be furious, of course.

Of course. After another moment, I add, Mind that this new fellow doesn't come to treat you like the old one.

She smiles dreamily. He would never.

I stay out on Saturday on purpose, lingering in the shops, ordering a few things I don't need and can't afford, eating supper alone at an inn. It's unlike me. I ponder what will be expected of me when I get home. Her things will be missing. Will the husband come to any other conclusion? That they've been robbed, that she was kidnapped? Would he be so fanciful, so blind? Is the boy in the cap a shared acquaintance? Will he know to go to him, pounding on his door, demanding the return of his property? At what point will the police get involved? Will my house become a place of scandal, and will that help or hurt my search for tenants?

When I return to the house, the entryway that links the front door and the stairs is pitch dark. With practiced hands, I light the handheld lamp on the table against the wall and carry it with me as I ascend.

(In this life, my life, an antique oil lamp decorates a high shelf, out of the toddler's reach, pretentious and useless.)

The husband must have left to begin his search. Among the heady bouquet of scents in the poorly ventilated house, competing with the kerosene of my lamp, is a new, faintly metallic smell—rust, iron. Passing their room, I notice the door is just the slightest bit ajar; he didn't bother to close and lock it in his hurry to leave.

I can't resist. I push the door open with one hand, the lamp in the other.

Their curtains are open. The streetlamps outside barely penetrate the gloom, which is broken only by the small circle of light and stark shadows produced by my lamp. The room is in disarray. I notice a small jewelry chest overturned onto the floor because the scattered baubles glint when touched by the lamplight. The large lump on the rug in the center of the room resolves into a sprawled human shape. The husband.

He's lying on his belly, his head turned to the side, his eyes open and glistening in the same way as the costume jewels. I stand in the doorway and guess at what happened: the husband came home early to discover the two lovers packing his wife's possessions. There was a scuffle with the blond fellow and the husband lost.

My eyes adjust fully, and I can make out more details. The smashed lamp on the floor by his head, which must have been unlit, otherwise it would have torched the place. The circular rug beneath him is soaked, saturated—a stain extends farther than its edges. A lock of dark, curly hair is clutched in his rigid fist, skin still attached to the roots. And then I spot it. A large hair ornament, half a foot long, pinchbeck and steel in the style of gold, likely from their wedding, likely the finest thing she owned—its pronged comb and razor edge in the shape of a leaf embedded in his side at an upward angle, held in place by his weight.

It was her, then. Young, but not in the way I thought. What strength it would have taken to pierce his skin with such a trinket, what adrenaline and mortal fear and hatred.

My mind drifts to other things. The ruined rug. The floor-boards that will need scrubbing, exactly how much blood has seeped between them, if it will forever darken the seams. The ghoulish voyeur who will likely be my next tenant, eager to be near tragedy, to have its vapors seep into his dreams.

In this fantasy, I wake up without an alarm around five a.m, in a cabin shrouded in the darkness of the surrounding woods. I pull the cord on a bare bulb that hangs in the kitchen, set stove-top coffee to boil. In the mudroom, I layer on a scarf, a fleece-lined plaid jacket, a toque, work gloves, and then head outside to chop wood for the backup stove. Where I live, the power is spotty and the nights are a killing cold. The wood splits easily; the water that seeped into the cracks has frozen, making the logs shatter at the seams upon impact. Clouds of my breath reflect the light off the snow, itself reflecting the still-present moon. I exhale with each axe swing, a loping rhythm with a thrilling moment of suspension: rise, arc, fall.

(In this life, I am not strong enough to safely lift an axe over-head. I haven't checked the earthquake kit in a few years, and I'm fairly sure the food and medication have expired. The last time a transformer blew, we went out into the street and stood blinking, dumbfounded, with neighbors from unlit buildings up and down the block, before taking refuge in a Starbucks.)

I come back inside just as the coffee is finished, stomp the snow from my boots. With my coffee, I read a book of poetry very slowly, lingering over each page for several minutes. The only person I have seen in months runs a general store thirty miles away, and we just nod over the counter.

At daybreak, I walk into the woods. I gather highbush cranberries into an old coffee can, idly chewing on pine sap pried from a trunk. I walk along a ridge and the valley below me, filled with snow, is lined with the pale pink and violet-blue edges of sunrise.

I enter an open clearing, and the sheen on the snow that melted and refroze overnight is blinding. On the opposite side of the clearing, less than a hundred feet away, stands a wolf. It takes two steps forward and stops, stands tall, gazing plainly in my direction, making clear that it has seen me as I have seen it. It's a beautiful creature at close range, healthy-looking, thick fur, silver-backed with a white mask and belly, amber eyes, pricked ears—though its fearlessness, its daring to approach me this way, is a sign that it's not well.

(Our incontinent eight-pound dog needs to be carried outside six times a day.)

In this fantasy, I am the kind of person who straightens her spine to grow larger, who knows not to run, who meets power with power. (Who doesn't begin an email about a six-months-overdue invoice with "Sorry to bother you.") I am someone who knows that the wolf will decide how this encounter ends. Who appreciates this presence, this sight, for the gift that it is, and meets without hesitation whatever fate may come.

In this fantasy, I am a princess on the morning of the revolution. Slightly dim-witted, bred and raised for acquiescence, contented and pampered like show cattle. I wake in my canopy-covered bed and only one of my three maids is there, the other two having fled in the night, along with half the staff. Our servants will be seen as longtime collaborators, stooges, bootlickers, enemies of the people. Some stay because they believe it is the safest choice, some out of a Stockholm syndrome–like loyalty, some because they've never known anything else.

She bathes me in the bathtub by the window. We are on one of the highest floors of the palace, facing the inner courtyard and the tittering dovecote, but we can still hear the rabble in the distance, the mob that has encroached upon the outer walls. As though it were any other morning, she massages lavender oil into my scalp, milky almond oil into my ephemerally pale skin, my unused muscles supple as raw veal, my brow uncannily blank and expressionless. Not beautiful, per se—more like a woman-sized baby, marvelously preserved. No one has ever asked me to think or make a decision. We hear a high-pitched shriek echo from somewhere else in the palace, the din from outside developing the regular, drumlike rhythm of chanting and marching. The distinctive tinkling crash of windows being broken.

After she ties me into my underlayers and gown—I wouldn't know how to get them on and off if I had to—the maid curtsies and hurries out. I float daintily, regally, through the hall connecting my bedchamber and my private sitting room. One of the paintings is askew, another missing, tucked under the arm of an absconding servant, leaving behind a square patch of brighter wallpaper.

In my sitting room, my breakfast has been laid out as usual. Exotic fruits, vibrantly colored as jewels—so ripe the flesh is nearly bursting through the skin, or candied, macerated, glazed to a mirror-shine. Thumb-sized pastries, sugar whirls drawn with a pin. Drinking chocolate, porridge with sweet cream, pickled vegetables, blue-speckled boiled eggs, smoked fish and meat with mustard. Nearly enough food for the starving rabble outside, from which I will, as every morning, idly pick a few bites and leave the rest to spoil.

I sit in a large, overstuffed armchair facing the door. I arrange my skirts, spreading them neatly over the edges of the chair, my slippered feet sinking into the sumptuous carpet. Hanging tapestries warm the walls, celestial scenes that will be treasured in museums for centuries to come. I am aware that I'm about to die. I have been kept almost entirely away from pain and violence, from complex sensation, from ordinary people who I now imagine will tear me apart like dogs. I feel the relief of a debtor releasing coins from his fist—a weight lifted, no longer beholden. Just imagine it: no longer feeling guilty for everything you have and don't deserve, for an unjust world bent in your favor, paying the piper at last. Wasn't it worth it, after all? My head on a pike for this sweet, short, pleasure-drenched life.

Sometimes, in my fantasies, I just disappear. Not in any way that I could—I don't get in our car and drive away, I don't follow a stranger into a club bathroom, I don't abandon my children in the grocery store. I sing a grand finale song-and-dance number, the audience hidden past the footlights. The timpani drum rolls, deep but buoyant, as ten thousand sequins sewn by hand glitter across my corseted bodice and mermaid skirt, as we belt out goodbyes the night before the theater becomes a parking lot. I journey through the stars, fingers trailing through cosmic dust, the unfeeling desolation of space. I sink through a fizzing, golden ocean, bubbles drifting past, gently dissolving my skin. I lie on clean, crisp sheets in a comfortable set of pajamas, buttons and drawstring, as a reassuring weight bears down on both of my shoulders and forces them apart, spreads and flattens my body out like dough, thinner and thinner, into a dun-colored sheet of pastry, into a single-layer matrix of atoms, and finally into the infinitely small that is indistinguishable from nothingness.

SCISSORS

As the curtains open, Dee sits on an empty stage in a small, cabaret-style theater. Black-painted walls, the smell of dust burning on the stage lights, ancient cigarette smoke baked into blue velvet drapery. The spotlight swings to Dee, a garish full moon. She sits in a plain wooden chair, her wrists bound to the armrests and her ankles to the chair legs with neatly torn strips of canvas. Her posture is slumped and casual, her knees open and her shoulders expansive and angled slightly backward, as though lounging in a hot tub. Her white T-shirt dress rides up over her thighs, the radiant heat on her bare arms and legs more like sunlight than moonlight.

The audience sits crowded around tightly packed, circular tables. Lit candles at the center of each one illuminate white tablecloths and sweating highball glasses, while the faces beyond remain largely in shadow. A table in the front row draws Dee's attention: a group that remained rowdy after a hush fell over the rest of the room, the only people she can see clearly in the reflected footlights. Their drinks slosh out of their glasses as they make jokes and jostle for the best view, but one person at their table is quiet, sitting back in his chair, slightly outside the conversation. He toys nervously with the candleholder, testing the hot glass, the tiny flame rolling on its wick. His hands jerk away and draw back. He glows pink, already blushing behind a pair of square glasses.

El enters stage left, dressed in a fitted tuxedo with tails, the black bow tie locking in place her high-necked shirt collar. She crosses in front of Dee. She holds up a pair of scissors, ordinary but large, stainless steel from tip to handle, as one might keep in the kitchen to snip through tendons and butcher twine. The steel catches the spotlight like a wink. She waves them around and gestures toward the audience, a magician with an empty hat.

El usually wears dagger pumps with the suit, six inches of killer heel, her trouser legs jacked up short. Tonight, she's barefoot. Dee stares. She's thrown by the sight of El's feet, their unexpected intimacy, her unpainted toenails like a row of pink pearls.

El grasps the bottom hem of Dee's dress and begins to snip. She takes her time. An inch, a pause. Another inch. The sound is satisfying, the neat clip of the blades coming together, the fabric stretching and shearing. A straight slice up the center, in line with Dee's navel. Dee feels the scissors close and stop at her solar plexus, and then El steps away. The fabric on either side of the split hangs to her sides like a flyaway nightgown, an inverted V of exposed skin between.

El leans in and kisses Dee on the mouth. Dee draws back, to the extent that she can, but El presses forward, the kiss soft and insistent. El has never kissed her onstage before. In the dressing room afterward, yes, during the frenzied, private fucking that used to end all of their show nights, El's sweat-melted makeup smearing across Dee's neck. She can't stop thinking about El's missing shoes. Her giantess persona shrunken to everyday height. Maybe it's nothing. Maybe a heel snapped backstage, moments before El's entrance, but Dee likes everything just so. Her surrender is an act of choreography. She can't do this if she's picturing El at home in her apartment, an apartment like any other. El taking off her shoes in a foyer and rubbing her tired arches, her blistered soles. El eating a bagel standing up in her kitchen, her bare feet on the linoleum.

Someone at the rowdy front table starts booing, but good-naturedly, still laughing. Get on with it! Don't tease us! Dee tries to focus on the audience, reorient herself in the moment. Her pupils have adjusted, and when she squints, she can see a couple at the very back, delineate their shapes from the darkness. Two women, their skin and pale hair lit red under the fire exit sign. They're making out distractedly—lazy groping with their attention drifting back to the stage, always one eye on Dee.

El snips through the last few inches of Dee's dress, now cut through from bottom to top. The edges curl outward, hanging over her bare torso like an unbuttoned jacket. When El tucks the flaps back and around her, the sleeves still comically intact, Dee can feel the energy in the room change. El steps back. She doesn't touch Dee. Nothing touches her, which makes the nakedness stranger, more acute, more helpless.

El taps the scissors against Dee's knee, as though absent-mindedly toying with a pen, exaggerating the bounce. She rests the point against the side of Dee's neck. The front table finally quiets.

El surveys Dee's body for a long moment, as though deep in thought, a vein jumping in Dee's throat. She lifts the scissors and presses the flat edge firmly against Dee's left breast, parallel to her body. Not piercing or cutting her, just sinking in, as into a mattress. A presence, a hardness, the potential of menace. Drawing attention to how soft she is, how her flesh indents and depresses to the slightest pressure. Nearly flush with her chest, the blades open and shut without catching any skin between them, snipping through air between her collarbone and nipple, severing an imagined connection.

The closed blades slip across and between her breasts, down to her belly, without a scratch, pressing and skimming like the back of a fingernail. Down farther, to the plushest part of her thigh. The steel begins to warm.

Dee loves the way the audience flinches at El's every movement. Their held breath. Gritting their teeth and clenching on the inside, holding as still as they can, as though if they don't move, if they don't exhale, Dee won't get cut. She knows it's maddening to watch, a sharp edge near skin, on skin, the tension of it, the blood pulsing inside all of them, swelling up like balloons that want to be popped. It's easier to be her, she thinks. She knows precisely where the scissors are, can feel the calm and control in El's grip. She feels as though her skin lifts to meet the metal of its own accord, faint hairs and gooseflesh rising, a slow, magnetic draw.

The scissors are flat against her stomach again, pointing downward, dipping now and again into the waistband of her underwear, colder on the concealed skin. El rotates them slowly until they're perpendicular to Dee's body, still pointing to her center.

The blades open, the beak of an eager bird. El snips through the side seams, the elastic at each leg opening, and the front half of Dee's underwear falls forward like a drawbridge. Dee strains against her bindings to lift her butt as El pulls the silky scrap away.

The low stage puts her knees at eye level of the crowd. If they don't raise or lower their gaze, it lands straight between her legs.

El uses the scissors to lift Dee's chin. Their eyes meet, lock. Now El is running the scissors along Dee's body without even looking down, blades all the way open in a narrow X, skimming in long sweeps as though curling ribbon. Her skin pinkens in strips from the friction and heat, though it remains unbroken. Her mind is still clear, serene, trusting, but her body clenches all the same, bearing down with her hips on the chair.

Still without looking, still on instinct, El touches the flat surface of the scissor blades—glancingly—to Dee's vulva, against the outer lips, and someone in the audience moans, a sound of simultaneous dread and desire. The steel is wet. She brings the blades together, only an inch from Dee's tenderest skin, the empty *snip* loud in the pin-drop silence. The same moan emerges from the dark.

El brings the scissors to Dee's mouth, prompting her to kiss them, which she does. She slips the pointed tip between Dee's lips, and Dee draws the closed blades deeper, up to the pin of the pivot point. The scissors feel dull against her palate and tongue, the depth of her mouth filled with metal. Dee is in control of this part, the sword swallowing, bobbing her head and sliding her lips. She looks up at El, pleased with herself, expecting El's eyes to be glassy with approval and desire, that wild-horse energy of hers, impatient for the next thing, for more.

But El isn't even looking at her. Her gaze is just beyond Dee, into the sea of candles and stained tablecloths. Her hand around the scissors relaxes, goes slack. Is she *bored*? Dee lunges upward, indignant, her mouth widening to take in the base of the handles, the tip in the opening of her throat. Without turning her head, she tries to see what's stealing El's attention. The hecklers at the front table? El is smiling in their direction the way she does when someone challenges her, presents her with a bet or a dare.

El takes the spit-polished scissors and cuts a strip from Dee's dress. She holds the scissors between her own teeth as she folds the strip in half, to thicken it, and wraps it around Dee's head as a blindfold. Blackness closes around her. Dee tries to trust what she knows: El tying a tight, neat knot at the back of her head; El tucking the scissors ostentatiously into her own hair, pulled back in a bun, like decorative chopsticks. A thrilling dread alights in her gut.

"Are you ready?" El stage-whispers.

Dee is supposed to pause and then nod shyly, to appear hesitant but excited. She's surprised to find herself actually hesitating. She told El from the beginning that she needed to write the details of her own submission, and El had understood. That Dee needed to be in control to give up control. That she would tap out over something as small as missing shoes, an unplanned kiss, an unnerving smile. That their lives had to be separate, their roles pure, their daytime selves left at the alley door of the theater. As though a hundred nights of sex and conversation and show adrenaline hadn't revealed more than any other relationship she'd ever had.

El has never nicked her onstage, never misjudged a fraction of an inch and drawn blood. The scissors remind Dee of a jangling, dubiously constructed roller coaster at the state fair near where she grew up. The two-person car held her loosely as the metal sides bruised her ribs and her head whipped back and forth on her spine. She'd once chipped her front tooth on the safety bar. But she was never truly afraid. She lined up over and over, elated.

The room is humid, hypnotized, heavy with want. In this moment, there's no acute danger, no dips and turns rattling her teeth in her head, no steel edge digging into her naked skin, yet she feels a vertiginous tingling through her fingers and toes. Her carnival fear edged with something real: El, her El, bored with her. What a bored El might do.

El puts her hand on top of Dee's, trapped palm side up on the armrest, and squeezes lightly in a gesture Dee understands: *It's all me. It's only me. It's always me.*

Dee nods.

"She says she's ready!" El cries, turning toward the audience. "Those who want to play, line up in an orderly fashion. Stay close to the wall and wait until I gesture for you to come forward. Remember, hands only, and your turn is up when I make this signal. We won't have time for everyone. I'll be watching! Rule breakers will be escorted out!"

Dee reminds herself that nothing is happening, that the murmuring and shifting and patter is for show, people are just heading to and from the bar—this has all been explained to them in advance. Dee's brain tells her one thing, that she's a performer in a well-established show with rules of her own making, while her body knows only that it's trapped, blinded and bound, the prickling sensation of being watched. Being seen without seeing. Even when she wasn't blindfolded, she'd been able to make out only a handful of faces—the shy man at the front table and his raucous companions, the couple under the exit sign. She has no idea who's out there. If they look hopeful, worshipful, like supplicants before a queen. If they're laughing, having a fun night out, amused by the whole situation. If they're sneering, impatient, eerily focused, blackout drunk. If they know her from some other time and place. A crowd is more lawless and unpredictable than any one person. A crowd is one of the most dangerous things she can think of.

Behind her blindfold, she pictures El's face, broad-browed, impish, easy to love. Dee remembers an evening, not long ago, when she arrived at the theater and found El in a loose-knit sweater with one sleeve, a ragged skein of wool dangling from her other shoulder. Dee thought that she'd been attacked, but El only laughed in astonishment. She'd been idly tugging on a loose thread, scarcely aware of what she was doing until she'd unraveled the entire sleeve. "I get fidgety when I'm bored," she said.

It's all me. It's only me. It's always me.

The first touch is a jolt. The tip of a fingernail grazing the back of her neck. She hadn't realized that anyone was behind her. The nail is pointed and sharp, the same intimation of threat as the scissors. She pictures a woman with brightly colored acrylics, stiletto tips. Large, teased hair, a bandage sheath dress. The fingers spread and comb upward through Dee's hair, palming the back of her head like a basketball, manicured claws flexing open and closed. Dee leans into it. She likes having her scalp scratched this way. El knows that.

The hand withdraws, immediately replaced by the sensation of touch on her sternum, slight enough to be chilling, ghostlike. An almost unpleasantly light touch, trickling downward, circling one nipple with a hesitancy that makes her tense. If there were wet paint on these fingers, they'd hardly leave a stain, the contact is so glancing. It seems clumsy, hungry, a little afraid, like a virginal teenage boy. The man with the glasses at the front table comes to mind. (Had El noticed him too? Is this her imitation of him?) The hand is joined by another, cupping her breasts from the front, and she imagines him standing in front of her, his glasses fogged with sweat, his shirt collar rumpled, his mouth falling slightly open, awed by the sight and feel of her. "That's enough," El says. Leaning back, throwing her voice in that way she does. She hears someone reluctantly stepping away before tweaking Dee's nipple in a spiteful goodbye.

Just as suddenly, someone grabs Dee by the neck, thumb and forefinger holding Dee's chin from below, the flat of their palm against Dee's throat. The movement is swift and sure, and Dee gasps. A little louder than necessary. The hand seems too large to be El's, the middle finger reaching almost to the back of her neck, the base of the wrist resting on her chest. Too slender and too smooth to be El's, missing her lifetime of calluses. Dee's mind draws a pianist's hand, wide-palmed with long fingers, masterful in its manipulation, octave to octave.

The musician gives her throat a friendly squeeze, the way you'd squeeze someone's upper arm in congratulations or comfort—except it's a flash of constriction, a skipped breath. El would never risk letting someone else touch Dee this way. Would she? A firmer squeeze. Dee gasps again without meaning to.

It's all me. It's only me. It's always me.

Her throat is released. Two hands settle on her thighs from the front. Someone is kneeling in front of her, close enough that Dee can feel their breath hot between her legs. They turn their head back and forth, blowing a stream of air from the inside of Dee's knee, up the inside of her thigh, across her pussy, down her other thigh, and back again. This, Dee thinks, seems like it violates the hands-only rule, in spirit if not word. The kneeler giggles, voice high and girlish. El's natural laugh is a big, spirited bark.

Strong hands massage the muscles at the base of her neck, unmistakably El's. Dee tells herself that El—somehow—stood from where she'd been kneeling and moved behind the chair without making a sound, without disturbing Dee's kinesthetic sense of where she was in the room. She tells herself it's El she feels looming over her, that the clatter of footsteps and the scent of unfamiliar sweat and cologne is farther away than it seems. She tells herself it's just El pretending to be other people, tricking the audience into thinking she's tricking Dee, as they've agreed.

She tells herself El would never turn her over to a roomful of strangers. Not even if Dee wanted her to. Not even if Dee begged her to. If Dee welcomed them, offered herself up like a feast. If she felt drunk on their attention, power-mad, giddy at having reduced a packed theater to single-minded animals.

Hands slide over Dee's shoulders, across her belly. Hands squeeze her breasts, climb up her thighs, rest on her hip, slap her cheek, tap the tip of her nose, tug lightly at her pubic hair. Hands palm her ass, cup her mound from behind. Fingers strum and abandon her clit. Fingers pop in and out of her mouth. Quick, darting motions, from all directions, never lingering, like she's swimming with a school of fish, at the lightless bottom of the sea. An overwhelming, disorienting, untraceable amount of touch.

It's just El, of course. Of course. El walking in circles around her, El and her ventriloquism, her disguises, her multiplying, quicksilver hands, able to reach every part of Dee at once. El, who knows her, who can give and take and break her. Or not. Dee will never know, not really, what happens to her as she swims in darkness—she will always have to take El's word for it. Dozens of times on this stage, she believes it was only El, only El's hands that she's ridden and bitten and bucked against, but she can't know.

And it's the not-knowing that makes her core sing.

Maybe people lined up in a theater, out the door and down the block, for the privilege of touching Dee, and it's these faceless figures who are grasping at her now, entering her with their hands, jostling for their turn. Maybe this time, El will lose control of the crowd, and they'll rush the stage, overwhelm her, a force as tremendous as Dee is powerless, strapped naked to a chair, her skin thrumming, death-defying adrenaline electrifying her veins.

Or.

Or El will whisper to Dee in her true, private voice, remove the blindfold, and reveal just the two of them onstage. She'll undo Dee's restraints, help her out of the chair, hold her upright on wobbling legs. She'll take Dee's hand, in her warm, familiar grasp, and raise their arms together, Dee still naked and bruised and soaked and spent, the audience beaming in the seats they never left, wild with applause.

JUNE BUGS

1.

Martha followed her new landlady, Mrs. Cutler, up the narrow flight of stairs along the left-hand wall of the foyer. She minded her feet, as the steps were ominously steep and irregular, and she was dragging a suitcase that now carried everything she owned in this world. Dust kicked up from the carpet runner nailed down the center of the stairs, dark red with a zigzag white design at the edges that reminded Martha of a Christmas sweater.

Martha had taken an intercity bus to a gas station/chicken restaurant forty minutes away, where Mrs. Cutler had picked her up. A neon light in the shape of a chicken head in profile was glowing in the window, though it was not quite dusk, and the smell of fryer grease inflected the hot, dry air. She watched the bus drive on without her, a streak of silver on the flat horizon, on a two-lane road that continued straight and unyielding to the edge of the earth.

She was free.

It was a long sunset, the deep blue remains lingering even as they pulled up to the house in Mrs. Cutler's truck. Mrs. Cutler introducing herself as such, as "Mrs.," could have seemed quaint, of a particular time, if Mrs. Cutler hadn't been so brusque and severe—more likely, she used the title to keep tenants from becoming overly familiar. Martha had rented the house based on one photo of the exterior. The house was witchily narrow and pointed, a faded mint green with white trim, the porch enclosed more recently into a sunroom off the living room and a mudroom off the front door.

At the landing at the top of the stairs, Mrs. Cutler gestured at the three doors hanging ajar, their contents lost to darkness. "Bedrooms, bathroom. The other bedroom is downstairs." Martha nodded. "I should tell you," Mrs. Cutler continued, "I'm going out of town for a couple months. I'm going in for surgery, and then I'll be staying with my son. So I'll need those postdated checks." When Martha appeared to hesitate, Mrs. Cutler added, "Like we agreed on the phone."

"What do I do if something goes wrong with the house?"

"My friend Barb lives next door. The white house, looks just like this one. She can get in touch with me or my son. But you won't need to. This house has survived plenty of winters. No reason why it should fall down during this one."

Winter had been far from Martha's mind. It was the first of October, after one of the hottest Septembers on record. She took out the envelope of checks she'd prewritten. Mrs. Cutler fingered through them as deftly as a casino dealer through betting chips.

Once she was alone, Martha wandered room to room. The hard surfaces were sticky and the soft surfaces were dusty; the best-before date on the cornstarch in the pantry was several years past. The promised washing machine was new enough to be front-loading, but a pan of stagnant water in front let her know that it leaked. There was a set of pots in the kitchen, thin aluminum bottoms and black plastic handles, a frying pan too dented and pitted to sit flat on the burner, and she felt a pang for the Dutch oven and cast iron she'd left behind. But everything could be cleaned, or fixed, or replaced over time.

The next morning, as Martha walked back from the grocery store, where the cashier had given her the long, knowing stare reserved for someone new in town, the sky loomed low, bright and colorless as steel. The plastic bag handles dug into the dry skin of her hands and she made a mental note to acquire a canvas tote somewhere. In her old life, tote bags had appeared out of the ether, multiplying in the coat closet on their own. She felt chagrined at how much it cost to set up even a furnished home from scratch, dish soap to toothpaste.

She came out of her own thoughts when she realized it was snowing. She stopped where she stood, nearly home—in front of Barb's house. Fat flakes melted as they touched her uncovered hair, kissed the warm asphalt of the road. The white house had the original porch, had been recently painted, and was all around in better condition than the one Martha was renting. She noticed someone in the living room window, watching Martha or the snow or both. She went inside.

The snow continued all day. Nearly all of the windows had heavy velvet drapes, maroon with yellow tasseled tiebacks, pile caked together by dust. The kitchen was the sole exception, with a sheer white panel that looked hand-sewn, tacked right to the frame above the table where Martha drank her coffee and ate her meals. Snow stuck scantily to the grass outside, like patches of lace.

She set up her computer and headset on a desk in the upstairs bedroom she hadn't slept in. The internet connection was surprisingly fast and consistent, considering how the water ran brown if she opened the tap too wide, how far away the bus stopped.

Flurries were still falling when she went to sleep. The next morning, it was like the snow had been a dream. Yellow grass and bare earth exposed, the damp burning fast away. Vibrant autumn colors clogged the gutters and held lightly to the trees, tinting the sunrise, another hot day beginning to reveal itself.

Downstairs, setting quick oats to boil in one of the cheap pots, she noticed a bug on the ceiling. A tiny beetle, its rounded back the size of her pinkie fingernail. Rust-colored, like the dowdy cousin of the ladybug. As she watched, it traveled across the ceiling until directly above her oatmeal, where it appeared to fall—or dive—straight down, landing silently, weightlessly, in the bubbling gray mush. She dug the boiled bug carcass out with a spoon and tossed it in the trash. Though she ate all of the oatmeal, buried in cream and brown sugar, it felt tainted.

In the office upstairs, she noticed another beetle crawling up the cord of the standing lamp. It stumbled where the cord plateaued and entered the lamp, falling off the side and landing on the desk on its back. The hair-thin legs twitched in panic before it righted itself again. Clumsy, disoriented little things, she thought.

A faint buzzing led her to pull back the window curtain. Beetles speckled the glass—she counted eleven, scattered like stars. They vibrated in place, struggling to move up or down or pass straight through the window. Two lay dead on the windowsill. Another fell as she watched. Up close, she could see they had clear, evidently decorative wings folded on their backs.

She didn't bother killing them; it would be like shoving a crowd of lemmings off a cliff. She sat down to take her first call. "Thank you for shopping with ShopGlobal. My name is Martha. Who am I speaking with?" She listened. "How can I help you?" she said. "I'm sorry to hear that," she said. Four hours passed. She went to the bathroom, where three dead beetles floated in the foamy puddle around the hand soap dispenser. She swept them into the sink and ran the water.

The evening came on suddenly, while she was caught up in her work, until she was talking to the angry, invisible voices by the light of her monitor alone, a fuzzy corona at the bevel. A beetle crossed her screen and she flicked it away.

The house felt larger at night. She'd never had so many dark, empty rooms to herself. She turned switches on and off as she passed from the office to the landing, down the stairs, to the kitchen, always surrounded by the only light in the house. She thought of a mural painted on the cinder block basement wall of her childhood Sunday school, a modestly well-done reproduction by a local artist of *The Light of the World*. The mural had frightened her then, everything bleak and muted so Jesus's golden halo and lantern stood out starkly—the sky behind him a murky twilight blue, sponged and streaked with black, spindly bare trees. His cloak receded into shadow, his face downcast beneath his crown of thorns.

She chopped some vegetables for soup. She hunched over her food protectively as a handful of beetles wandered around the ceiling, moving radially toward the light fixture, a concave, flower-shaped chandelier, as though mesmerized. Several crossed the lip and fell into the bowl, tumbling down the curved sides. Their silhouettes were distinct, magnified by the light, legs and antennae and coffee-bean abdomens, and for the first time she felt worried, repulsed. She would have to borrow a ladder to take down the bowl and empty the carcasses.

She ate her soup and went upstairs. She startled a beetle that had been resting on the bedroom lampshade. She finished unpacking her suitcase. Her clothes barely filled half the drawers in the weathered pine wardrobe—a pale, uneven gray, the varnish worn off. She laid her jewelry box on the nightstand. She put her hairbrush in the bathroom. After some thought, she took the gun downstairs, still in its shoebox, where she put it on top of the refrigerator.

Martha woke and didn't know where she was. She thought it was the middle of the night, but when she checked her phone, it was nearly six. She decided to go for a walk before her shift.

Dressed and downstairs, she opened the inner door, the original front door. The step down into the mudroom, where she'd hung her coat and left her boots two days before, was covered with beetles. The living mixed with the dead. The motion of the door had launched a few of them airborne, sweeping them backward. Others crunched under her sock foot. The living beetles, dotting the walls and floors, moved in every direction, but the overall pattern converged at the door, at Martha's feet, like tributaries running to the ocean. Not just her feet, she realized—they were crawling up and around the doorframe, pulsing in the seam of the wood.

By the end of the week, Martha no longer went in the mudroom. The floor was a seething sea of beetles—their color of dried blood, the sheen of their glassy wings like cresting waves—that washed up and over the old front door. She went in and out through the back door of the kitchen. She'd never gotten to use the sunroom, where beetles now blotted out the skylights and tall windows, formed a second layer of upholstery on the cushioned chairs.

Two days in a row, she went to Barb's house around dinnertime and rang the bell. She thought she saw movement in the living room window, a ripple in the curtains—beige, light-weight, modern ones—but no one came to the door. On the third day, she tried at about nine in the morning; on the fourth, later in the evening; on the fifth, midday.

On the sixth day, she arrived just before seven a.m. and rang the bell repeatedly, letting the chimes interrupt each other. Loud, hurried footfalls and the sound of a dead bolt turning. The door opened a crack, still chained, revealing a sliver of an older woman's face. "Stop making that ruckus," she hissed. "My husband is sleeping."

"Barb?"

"Who wants to know?"

"I'm Martha, Mrs. Cutler's tenant next door. I'm sorry to come over so early, but I've tried several times, and it seems like you're never home."

"I don't answer the door for strangers."

"I understand, but Mrs. Cutler told me to contact you if I was having trouble with the house, and she didn't give me your phone number."

"Christ almighty." Barb closed the door slightly to undo the chain, and then opened it wider but made no gesture for Martha to come in. She looked so similar to Mrs. Cutler that Martha wondered if she'd misheard, and Mrs. Cutler had said "sister" rather than "friend." They had the same enviably thick hair, white as cotton and bobbed to the chin, the same long nose and narrow face, though Barb had brown eyes and Mrs. Cutler's had been blue, and Barb wore glasses. "What kind of trouble?"

"There's some kind of bug infestation in the old porch." Martha had a glass of beetles. She'd braved the mudroom for just long enough to scoop some beetles into the glass with a piece of paper. She held the paper on top of the glass now, but she knew from experience that even without it, the beetles wouldn't be able to climb the glass walls, nor would they deploy their wings to fly up and out.

Barb lifted her glasses to peer inside. "June bugs," she said. "Some people call them May beetles. Because they come out in late spring, early summer."

"It's October," Martha said.

"They probably got confused because of that freak snow. Have they gotten in the house?"

"Yes, here and there. But there's tons of them in the mudroom and the sunroom. Like ..." Martha gestured helplessly. She didn't know how to convey the living, writhing walls. "Hundreds, I think."

"Hundreds," Barb repeated skeptically. "Well, lucky for you, the cold will kill them or send them back underground soon enough." Barb let her glasses drop back down to her nose. "They don't bite or sting. They're harmless. You can pick them up with your bare hands and dump them outside, if they're bothering you."

The adrenaline that had led her to jab the doorbell over and over was subsiding. She'd come to demand an exterminator, and now she felt like she'd been silly, hysterical. "There's just . . . there's so many. Could you come over and see?"

"What am I going to do? Winter will be here soon enough. There's no heating in that porch add-on, so they'll all die in there. We don't need to bother Mrs. Cutler, in her condition. You know she's getting surgery? Just use the back door for now."

"I have been."

"Great," Barb said, with an air of finality, problem solved. She took a step back, deeper into her home. "You take good care of the house now," she added, closing the door.

Martha opened the utensil drawer in the kitchen and a beetle scurried out. She put her hands in her coat pockets and felt the crisp, dry dead, or the spiny protrusions on their legs as they scrambled up her fingers. When she went to shower, she noticed four beetles drowned in the thin skin of water that always remained over the tub drain. She turned on the shower to wash them away, and the beetles that had been standing upside down on the showerhead were blasted off.

It took her a while to realize that the curtains, being so dark and similar in color, hosted clusters of beetles in their folds. She tried vacuuming them out with the ancient, bagged vacuum she'd found in the house, but it quickly clogged. She went to the hardware store and bought sticky traps, which filled with beetles every night and had to be changed every morning. She went back and stared at aerosols and poisons, all intended for different bugs than these—these were harmless, after all—but they seemed pointless given the magnitude of the problem. Where would she spray? She'd have to tent and fumigate the whole house.

Because they were so slow and feeble, she eventually found the easiest thing to do was to scrape them off surfaces—the table while she ate dinner, the desk while she worked, the walls, windows, doors, shelves, counters, and in particular the blades of the ceiling fan above the upstairs landing, a favorite daytime resting place of theirs, which she could reach by standing on a chair—with a playing card, into a drinking glass, and once full, dump the glass into the toilet. She disposed of so many beetles this way she thought she would eventually get rid of them all, but instead there seemed to be more and more.

She finally went back to Barb one evening after dinner, who opened the door this time. Without greeting her, Martha said, "The June bugs are in the house."

"This again? I told you, they're harmless. You never saw bugs in the city?"

"You don't understand. They're everywhere. In my clothes. In my food."

"It's not their season. It's getting colder. You can feel it." Barb gestured out the door, the draft they were letting into her house. "They burrow and go dormant in the winter. They'll disappear on their own."

"Do you have them?"

"Me? No."

"Why not? Why is it only my house?"

Barb shrugged.

"Can we ask Mrs. Cutler if this has happened before? She might know what to do."

"No, no, no. We're not going to bother poor Mrs. Cutler unless her house is burning down, not while she's still in recovery," Barb said, shaking her head.

"Her son, then. She said she was staying with her son."

"That idiot? What's he going to do? I'll tell you what. If the June bugs are still there once the snow starts again—which they won't be—I'll come over and kill them all myself."

"I've been dumping them in the toilet, dozens of them, it makes no—"

Barb interrupted, horrified. "Christ, don't do that! These houses have old pipes. They clog easily." She had her hand on her chest, and she shook her head, as though in disbelief at Martha's idiocy. "Put them in the trash. Or just wait it out. June bugs eat plants. There's nothing in your house they want, other than the warmth. They'll freeze, they'll starve, or they'll disappear."

"Please, just come and see it. If you saw it, you'd believe me."

"I believe you. There are June bugs in your house. Why don't you believe *me*? I've been living here my whole life. The June bugs come, and the June bugs go. It's in their name."

The argument exhausted Martha. The sensation of shutting down, conceding to make it end, felt familiar. She trudged back to her own house, where the June bugs were waiting, the hum and scratch of their movements so soft and continuous it could have been inside her own head.

That night, as she washed her dinner dishes, and again when she brushed her teeth, she thought of all the beetles she had flushed, filling the old pipes, heaped row on row like skulls in a catacomb. She hesitated over the taps, picturing geysers of beetles shooting from backed-up drains, beetles pouring from the faucets.

It was bearable in the daytime, busy as she was with work and chores, the beetles mostly hidden, spread out across the house. The worst was the time between dusk—which fell earlier and earlier—and when Martha went to sleep, when they flocked to whatever room she was in, the sole break in the darkness, the light of their world. They gathered in her lit bedroom as she shook her pajamas out, usually dislodging a beetle or two, as she changed and got into bed, and then dispersed in their slow, aimless way once she turned out the light.

The nights grew colder. She kept the radiators off as much as possible, hoping the beetles, as promised, would finally freeze. One night, she was awakened by a beetle crossing her face. She lurched up, swatting it off, and discovered another beetle in her hair. She turned on the light. She combed through the bedding and found two more. Just as the bugs had been drawn into the enclosed porch, and then into the house, moving mindlessly toward warmth, they would now be drawn to *her*. They would confuse the lump of her under the heaped blankets for the sun-warmed topsoil they sought, the break in the universe where they could emerge into summertime.

She got up and went to the kitchen. She turned on the radiator full blast. She took down the shoebox. It contained not only the gun and cartridges but everything she'd bought while she was still hiding it: cotton patches, a barrel brush, spray solvent, lubricating oil, a cheap child-sized toothbrush. She laid out a kitchen towel on the table. She disassembled the gun. She spread out the components, hollow and light. The cleaning was unnecessary— the patches came out white, and she brushed away only a thin film of dust—but as soothing and meditative as it ever was.

At the end, she loaded the magazine, disengaged the safety, pulled back the slide to chamber the round. She used both hands to hold it, her elbows on the table like a tripod. She pointed the gun at the kitchen radiator, haloed by June bugs. A few sizzled on the surface, frying before they thought to move. She stared down the sight and pictured launching a small explosion into their world, June bugs flying in all directions.

2.

Five years earlier, Martha met Neil while leaving a party. She had been pleasantly, whirlingly drunk inside, but was sobered by the rush down the several flights of stairs between the host's apartment and the door to the street.

Martha had called for a cab, and the dispatcher told her fifteen minutes, so she'd stayed at the party for another fifteen minutes, or so she thought, until the cab company called back to say he was outside and didn't see her, so she'd hurried downstairs, turning back once when she realized she'd forgotten her coat. Now that she was standing at the curb, there was no cab in sight. No cars at all, in fact, just a man leaning on the brick wall of the building, to the left of the entrance, sucking on his cheeks and exhaling visibly in the cold air—the pose of a smoker, save his empty hands. She called the cab company back, and the dispatcher said he'd gotten tired of waiting and had taken another pickup. Should they send another?

The effort of getting down the stairs quickly without falling, her eyes heavy and her feet loose, dancing on their own, suddenly caught up to her. She felt very tired. The man pushed off the wall, stepped toward her, and plucked her phone out of her hand, the gesture more gallantry than theft. "Yes," he said into Martha's phone. "Send another cab. We'll wait right here this time." He hung up and handed it back to her. "May I share your cab?"

Martha stared at him, clutching her phone hard. She was conscious of blinking, her eyelids sticking together and peeling apart. "I'm headed uptown," she said.

"Great, me too. Are you coming from Jimmy's party?"

"Yes."

"He's such a piece of shit, isn't he?"

Martha relaxed. "Yeah, but he throws great parties."

"You think? Maybe I'm getting too old for parties." He was flicking the fingers on his right hand, one by one, with his thumb, forming an O with each finger in turn. "I'm Neil."

"Hi, Neil," she said, not offering her name in return. "Why are you just standing out here?"

"I quit smoking a few months ago. Four months, almost. It's the best I've ever done. I realized some of the problem is that I missed the ritual. The first cigarette in the morning, cig-arettes after meals, after sex, at the end of the night. So now

I stand outside of parties with a mint in my mouth, without biting, until the whole thing dissolves."

"And in the morning?"

"I stand on my fire escape with a cup of coffee that's too hot to drink, really scalding, and I blow on it and sip it until it's gone."

"And after sex?"

He smiled faintly. "That's a good question. It hasn't come up."

"Ever?" she teased.

"In the last four months."

"Are you quitting that too?"

He looked directly at her. "Definitely not."

She turned away, seeing headlights up the road. "There's the cab."

"There's our cab," he echoed.

The drive out of the old warehouse district where Jimmy lived passed through long blocks with streetlights placed far apart, and few other cars on the road at that hour, cocooning the back seat in darkness. Neil was about the same height as Martha, and a wisp of a person, an under-stuffed scarecrow with a sharp, beak-like chin, while she was wide in the shoulders and hips, her middle solid as a drum—but in the cab he seemed to loom larger, leaning over her. His mouth first in her hair and then on her mouth, one hand holding her chin in place, the other seizing her waist inside her coat.

At the beginning, she was embarrassed for herself in this story, their origin story. She didn't want people to know she let a man she'd just met kiss her, that she followed a man home after knowing him for only minutes. A couple of years later, a little older, she thought, who cares? There's nothing wrong with casual sex with a stranger, if everyone has a good time. Later still, she felt embarrassed for *Neil* in this story—what did it say about him, that he grabbed a woman he'd just met, in a moving car where she couldn't escape?

We were young, she'd think. And then she'd look at Neil, who dressed the same way all the years they were together, in faded band tees and distressed, low-slung jeans, and she'd think: Not that young. He wasn't that young.

But that kiss. She'd described it many ways, comforting Neil after fights, stroking his hair while he lay in her lap and pressed his face into her belly. Remember our first kiss? She'd never been kissed like that. So urgently, hungrily. Like the world was ending, she said. Like in the movies. Like all the clichés: fireworks going off in the background, her stomach dropping like she was cresting a hill on a roller coaster. She had never felt so acutely aroused from just a kiss, felt a kiss in the roots of her hair and the pulse of her crotch. In the retelling, she didn't mention that she was still drunk, or that his fingernail snagged on her wool tights and unraveled a fist-sized hole in the inner thigh, ruining them. Or that she kept mumbling that the cab driver could see them, how she got out with Neil at his apartment partially because she didn't want to be left alone with the driver after he'd caught a glimpse of her bare breast in the rearview mirror. Fireworks, she'd say. You were so beautiful, he'd reply. You were the most beautiful woman I'd ever seen.

Martha's lease was up when she'd only been dating Neil for two months, and when he suggested she move in, it made sense. They were together constantly.

About a year in, she came home and found Neil asleep on the couch. He should've still been at the record store where he worked, a job he loved—a job he'd had for ten years, since he was nineteen. There was only one other employee at a time besides Neil and the owner, teenagers who rotated in and out, taking a couple of shifts in the summer, while Neil worked eleven a.m. to seven p.m., six days a week. The owner had talked about passing on the shop to Neil when he retired. A coworker of Martha's once remarked, "Neil *looks* like he works at a record store," and Martha was never able to unsee it. Though he was only twenty-nine, he had the mien of an aging rock star: carved-out face, cartilage piercings, his hair stubbornly long in the back and curling short at the temples.

Their windows faced northeast, the apartment dark by midafternoon in the winter. She'd been looking forward to some time alone at home. She took off her shoes and put down her bag as quietly as she could, trying not to wake Neil.

He spoke without opening his eyes. "The store closed down. The whole block was bought by a developer."

She paused. She felt an urge to turn around and just leave again, to not have to deal with this, and then an aftershock of guilt. She stepped lightly toward him. In his sleep, his shirt had twisted and ridden up, and she noted for the first time in a while how thin he was, his jutting ribs and hip bones. His exposed bones made him look fragile, easily damaged, a raw nerve in the wind. She wanted to wrap herself around him, cushion him from the world. "I'm so sorry, babe."

"I don't know what I'm going to do."

She lifted his legs to sit down on the couch, lowering his feet onto her lap. "Rob's always saying they need people at the bar."

"I don't want to be a fucking bartender."

"You don't have to decide anything right now." She started massaging one of his feet. "It just happened. You can take some time to figure out what you want to do next."

"Sure, I can mooch off of you. I can be that guy. I'm sure you'd love that. I'm sure you'll still want to fuck me when you're paying the rent and I've been sitting on my ass all day."

She let his foot drop. "Why are you being so nasty?"

"Sorry. I'm sorry." He rubbed his face with both hands. "It's just . . . a shock."

Six months later, Martha found herself hesitating at her own door, standing in the outer hallway with her keys in hand. She'd gone to happy hour with her new ShopGlobal coworkers and ended up staying at the bar for hours, though she'd only had a couple of drinks. Their group had taken over the rear patio, which looked like someone's back garden, lush and overgrown. Untamed bordering bushes and stomped-down grass, a heavily lopsided apple tree surrounded by felled, split fruit. She picked one of the long, bowing stalks of English lavender that grew in rounded clusters behind their table, and crushed the flowers and stem between her hands, inhaling the scent. Their apartment grew dark and claustrophobic in her mind, nowhere she wanted to be. Especially as it got later in the evening, and the fairy lights threaded in the patio fencing came on, and she knew Neil would be angrier and angrier that she hadn't been responding to his texts or answering his calls, that she wasn't home on his night off.

She went inside. She could tell Neil had been pacing from the way he stood, interrupted mid-step. "I thought you were dead," he said flatly. "I thought you got hit by a bus. I was wondering when I should call the police. Why didn't you answer your phone?"

"I told you I was going to happy hour."

"I assumed that meant you'd be home before dinner."

"Oh, did you make dinner for once?" The barb slipped out before she could stop it.

He wrinkled his nose. "You're drunk."

"No, I'm really not."

"You reek of alcohol. You know I deal with drunk assholes every other night of the week. Now I have to do it on my night off."

"I had two drinks, Neil."

"Two drinks? You're telling me you had two drinks in, what, four hours? Five hours?"

Martha felt trapped between Neil and the apartment door behind her. She pushed forcefully past him. "I just didn't feel like coming home." She turned back and saw his expression crumbling, his eyes large and wounded. "Oh, Jesus. I didn't mean it like that. We were on the patio and it was a nice night. It felt good to be outside."

"You didn't want to come home to me."

"No, I . . ."

He shut his eyes and clutched his head. "You hate me."

"Neil, stop it." She held his wrists and forced his arms down. "You know that's not true. You know I love you. I love you."

"I love *you*," he said, his voice strained. "I love you so much."

They held each other for a moment, and then, still speaking very softly, he added, "Seeing all those idiots get fucked up night after night, barely aware of what they're doing, I worry about you."

"I don't drink like that."

"I'd rather you didn't drink at all." He released her from the embrace. "We could do it together. Go sober together."

"I'm not an alcoholic."

He waited a moment, as though making sure she'd heard herself. *I'm not an alcoholic*, the mantra of alcoholics everywhere. "It's not like drinking is healthy. It's basically poison. And the calories ..."

She pulled back. He held her firmly by the shoulders. "Don't you fucking—*calories*—" she sputtered.

His expression was affectionate, but his grip was hard, her flesh squeezing between his fingers. "I mean it's not good for either of us. It's not good for anyone. I'm not saying anything about your body."

She let out the breath she was holding, but her lungs still felt constrained, and her voice came out small and tight. Only alcoholics couldn't give it up. "Okay. Okay, let's quit drinking for a while."

During a fight a few months later, Neil pointed out that— during *this* fight—he'd never asked her to stop going to happy hour with her coworkers. She could have gone and had a selt- zer. As though he wouldn't still have been waiting and pacing like a confined animal. As though her coworkers wouldn't have asked why, and what would she say? My boyfriend thinks I'm an alcoholic, but I'm really not. Only alcoholics say that. If she said she just didn't feel like drinking, over and over, the office gossips would speculate she was pregnant. Well, Neil said, they certainly sound like people you want to hang out with, don't they?

She tried to explain, as kindly as possible, that sometimes she wanted to see people who weren't Neil, sometimes she wanted to be out and not have to worry about his feelings, where he was, if he was okay—and he cried, he was sorry, he just wanted to be with her all the time because he loved her so much, but she didn't love him, she must be so happy that he worked nights now and they barely saw each other—

And she held him, stayed up with him. Another night of sleep ruined, another bleary workday morning ahead. She said, to herself as much as to Neil, "Remember our first kiss?"

They were arguing about the dishes, standing in the kitchen, when Neil started in on his routine—she didn't love him, she must hate him—and for the first time, Martha didn't rush to reassure him. Her arms stayed at her sides, her expression blank. "Oh my God, you do," he whispered. "You do hate me." She couldn't summon the energy. She couldn't recite her lines in this skit they performed more and more often.

"You should just hit me," he said. He leaned in and offered his cheek, as though for a kiss. "You should hit me for being such a terrible boyfriend."

She walked out of the kitchen. He followed her, walking sideways, pushing his face at her, his voice rising in pitch, cracking like a boy's. "Go on, hit me! You obviously want to. You hate me so much. I can see it in your face."

She dodged around him as he jumped in front of her. "Just do it. I want you to do it. Do it! Hit me!"

She stared at the floor, trying not to look into his eyes, which had a frightening energy, his pupils dilated like he was high—ironic, as he'd long forbidden her from drinking or smoking weed. "Stop it," she said. He feinted around her like a basketball player trying to block her shot.

"Look at me," he demanded. "Look at me. Admit you hate me."

"Let me go."

"I'm not touching you."

The game of a child bully. Not touching you, not touching you. Cutting off her path, hovering over her with his arms out, trapping her between furniture as she stumbled, the heat-boil of her frustration. If only she could get to the bedroom or the bathroom, a room with a door. "Neil, stop it. Please stop."

"Come on. Hit me. As hard as you can. I want you to. I want you to hit me!" Screaming now. "Hit me, hit me, hit me!"

She tried to shove past him, pushing on his chest, knowing almost before she made contact that it wouldn't work, he wouldn't budge.

She was on the ground.

Had she tripped over something? Had she fallen?

Her right ear was ringing. She hadn't made a sound.

She gazed up at Neil. His face was filled with terror. She realized only then that he'd struck her. She guessed he'd meant to slap her with the back of his hand, but his aim was off, his fingers hadn't fully uncurled, and his knuckles caught the side of her head in a backfist. A punch. He'd punched her in the head.

He knelt beside her. He was crying. She wasn't, still lost to astonishment. Sobs racked his whole body. He pulled at his clothes as though trapped inside them, wailing like an animal. He tried to speak between ragged gasps. "I didn't—I'm so—I can't . . ."

She rose up on her knees beside him. She felt strangely calm, a kind of catharsis, an ending. The flood of his tears, like breaking open a dam. She embraced him, pulled his head to her chest, rubbed his back, murmured soothingly in his ear. He didn't mean to do it, he didn't mean to hit her so hard, she knew, she knew. She guided him to their bed. They held each other all night, like they'd survived together some external storm.

Treading carefully, sweetly, kissing around the tender goose egg on her temple. Corner store daisies waiting in a vase when she came home; she would have said she didn't like daisies, but she found herself moved by the burst of color, the new smell in the apartment, the air of change. He went down on her for an entire afternoon, solicitous and slow, building and retreating while she squealed in delight. Around this time, friends of Martha's whom she hadn't seen in years came into town, and when they all went out for dinner, they remarked on how cute she and Neil were together, how obviously in love.

The next time he told her to hit him, she did. She slapped him across the face. She could see the sting in his expression, and there was a bright, acidic taste in her own mouth, like biting into a lemon.

She was so used to thinking of him as weak, delicate, in need of her care. Thinking of herself as overly large, a great bulk of a person. It felt unreal, how swiftly he overpowered her, forced her to the ground. She remembered how that loss of power, the way he suddenly seemed different—bigger, stronger, more in control—had turned her on the night they met, in the cab. What would she tell her younger self now? He lifted her bodily by the wrists and dropped her, the back of her skull landing hard on the living room floor. Sparks flashed in darkness before her open eyes, a split-second blindness.

In the morning, she packed a bag. He begged her to stay. She stayed. Six weeks later, she packed and unpacked it again. Packed and unpacked. Packed and unpacked.

One morning that spring, Martha got a seat on the train—a rarity, as it was usually full by her stop. She checked her work email on her phone as the train continued through the tunnels, featureless holes with or without light. An unceremonious message announced that her entire division had been outsourced to a third-party company. In another email, the new company had already sent an offer to rehire her, but noted in sly, cheerful language that they had no physical office, full-time positions, or benefits. She'd be doing the same work—answering the customer service line for ShopGlobal—but she'd be doing it from home on a headset connected to her own personal computer, as a *contractor*, in shifts that would be assigned two weeks in advance. A bolded subheading promised *Freedom and Flexibility!*

She got off the train at the next stop, intending to cross the bridge to the other side of the track and ride home again. Halfway up the crowded, vertiginous stairs, her steps slowed to a stop. The person behind her pulled up short. Martha hugged the rail as people flowed around her, an island in a river, some cussing her out as they passed. "Get out of the way!" a woman cried.

She pictured going home, where Neil would still be asleep after his night shift. Telling him that she'd be working from home from now on. He would be jubilant. I'll be working, she'd say. I won't be able to pay attention to you. That doesn't matter, he'd say. I just want you to be around. I just want to be near you.

She exited the station. Emerging at ground level, she was across the street from the downtown police headquarters, a brutalist concrete and glass building with a large front plaza. White tents filled the plaza, and a line stretched from the tents down and around the block, consisting almost entirely of middle-aged white men, pinking in the heat. It was one of the first warm days that year, the sun bearing down unimpeded.

A small sign indicated that this joyless carnival was a gun buyback program. Staying on the opposite side of the street, Martha followed the line to its end, curious to see how long it went. She felt a rubbernecking excitement at the sight of a duffel bag bulging at sharp angles, instruments of war in unmistakably shaped cases.

The last man in line wore a winter-weight wool suit. He wiped sweat from his face with his sleeve. He glanced at his watch, sighed, shook out his shoulders, telegraphing his impatience. Martha crossed the street and strode up to him with purpose, as though they knew each other. Her feet were guiding her, as they had since the station, with the confidence and inevitability of a dream.

"How much do they give you?" she asked.

"A hundred-dollar ShopGlobal gift card for rifles, shotguns, and handguns," he said. "Two hundred for assault weapons."

She felt a twinge at the mention of her now-former employer. "What are you turning in?"

"My dad's semi. And some bullets. They don't give you anything for those, but they'll destroy them for you."

"Just the one?"

He mopped his face with his sleeve again. "Yes." He glanced at the people continuing to gather behind him, Martha's shoulder close to his own. The only thing the man carried was a library foundation tote bag, the blue logo and *Support Your Local Libraries* in stylized cursive. She pictured herself grabbing his bag and taking off down the street.

"What if I give you fifty in cash right now instead?" she said.

He looked directly at her for the first time. Slowly, he said, "It's worth a lot more than that."

"I'm not going to keep it. I'm going to take your spot in line and get the gift card." She marveled at the words coming out of her mouth, as smoothly as if she'd planned it in advance. "Fifty in profit for me, no more waiting for you. You seem like you're in a rush."

"This line is ridiculous," he said. "I didn't expect this."

"I don't have anywhere to be," she said. "It's a win-win."

He stared at Martha for a long moment. In a recent fight, Neil said it was her face that had made him snap—lately, he said, she stayed expressionless even when he was screaming at her, like she couldn't hear him, like she wasn't listening, like she didn't care. Afterward, he'd fucked her from behind as they lay on their sides, and in the mirrored closet door by their bed, she saw what he meant: her mouth and brow unmoved, her half-moon eyes placid and bovine, her face a pool of unreachable stillness.

"Sixty," he said. She took out three twenties from her wallet, and he handed her the tote bag, which lurched downward between them as she shifted her grip. "You can keep the bag."

She stood in line for as long as it took for the man to look both ways, hurry across the street, and disappear around the side of a building. As soon as he was out of sight, she stepped out of the line. She walked briskly, head up, staring straight ahead, for the three miles home. Her feet blistered against the thin, worn espadrilles she'd put on that morning, for an entirely different day.

At first, having it was enough. A talisman, a secret shrine. Knowing it was there, at the bottom of her plastic tub of out-of-season clothes, buried under sweaters or shorts, arranged in a shoebox: the unloaded gun, two boxes of cartridges, the tote bag rolled up neatly alongside. She called it "the gun" in her head, not referring to make, model, or caliber, as though it were the only gun in the world—a childish solipsism, like naming a dog Dog.

One night, Martha had trouble falling back asleep after Neil came home and joined her in bed. Their bedroom window was open to another unseasonably warm night, cottonwood fluff blowing in and somersaulting across the floor. She thrashed in the sheets. Her skin felt hot to the touch.

She went into the bathroom and turned on the light. Hives speckled her forearms. She lifted her shirt and saw the same raised welts across her stomach.

"What are you doing?"

Neil had snuck up behind her, shadowy in the dark hallway.

"I have a rash or something," she said.

"Let me see."

She didn't want to show him. She wanted him to go away. She held out one of her forearms.

"Do you think we have bedbugs? Or fleas? Maybe I brought them home from the bar."

"It doesn't look like that. It's probably just allergies."

He cradled her wrist in his palm. "Do you want me to run to the all-night drugstore?" he asked. "Get you some Benadryl or calamine lotion?"

She felt bad for her petulance. Neil could be so sweet, so thoughtful. He loved to take care of her. "No, you just got home and settled in. Go get some sleep. I can go myself."

He still held her wrist lightly, both of them gazing down at the red spots on her arm. In the long pause before he answered, the spots were joined by goose bumps, the hair on her arm rising, knowledge in the body before the mind. "Why won't you let me do this for you?"

"I was just—"

"You always do this. You won't let me do something nice for you, and then later you'll complain that I didn't help." His grip tightened, pressing down on the rash.

"That hurts," she said.

He let go, stepping back and holding up his hands dramatically, as though—she couldn't avoid the thought—she were pointing a gun. "I was barely touching you."

The white imprints of his fingers and the surrounding flush where he'd squeezed her arm dissipated in the space of a breath. "I don't think I need anything, babe," she said, not looking up. "Let's just go back to bed."

The following evening, after Neil left for his shift, Martha took out the gun. She held it and examined it up close. With its matte, plasticky finish and hollow weight, it seemed almost fake—a toy or a prop gun. The feel of the grip and the trigger guard brought to mind a small kitchen appliance, a rice cooker or a microwave. An everyday machine, push-button modern ease. Her late father had inexplicably hated microwaves. He'd claimed microwaved food tasted contaminated. "Some things," he'd said, "shouldn't be rushed."

Handling the gun left a faint residue on the pads of her fingers, like touching newsprint. She wasn't sure if it was carbon or just dust and grime. She Googled her gun—the gun—and watched a video of someone disassembling and cleaning it, the same top-down view of disembodied hands on a worktop as in most online cooking videos.

Cleaning and oiling the gun at the kitchen table became her new ritual, a touchstone after each fight with Neil, the next time she was alone. She did it slowly and deliberately, enjoying the smooth, puzzle-like way the components fit back together when she was done. Her former supervisor at ShopGlobal had kept a miniature Japanese rock garden on his desk, no bigger than Martha's, and would rake the sand while on the phone—it was like that, she thought. It was something else when she learned to load it. Stacking ammunition in the magazine, one by one. Reinserting the magazine and hearing the click. She felt a sickening wave up the back of her spine and her hands trembled, like the first intimations of a flu. At any moment, she might blow a hole through the table or her foot. How few things in her life had frightened and thrilled her this way—masturbating as a child, speeding on the highway as a teenager. In all cases, a power she felt she shouldn't have.

She could have walked into a sporting goods store and plunked down a few hundred dollars and her ID, waited out the days. She lived in a nation in which guns were readily at hand, clear-cutting lives, a litany to face each day. Instead she had conned someone doing the right thing. She could take a class at a shooting range in wraparound goggles and earmuffs. There were classes just for women. There were ladies' nights. Instead these faceless hands on the internet, narrating the steps in hushed tones, as though there were a sleeping baby or wife in the next room as he filmed. She felt connected to the low timbre and distinct twang of his voice. What a time to be alive. She could learn anything, alone in her kitchen, in what felt like the increasingly rare moments she was alone, without anyone knowing. Just in case. In case what? She put down the loaded gun on the table, muzzle pointing toward the refrigerator. (Would the compressor explode?) She watched the gun as though expecting it to come alive, to speak to her, to make decisions.

Eventually, inevitably, Neil caught her. A week before, he'd thrown his own phone out their sixth-story window. A week before that, he'd hurled a drinking glass to the floor in frustration, and she'd broken a plate in response, and they stood and stared at each other, islands in this sea of broken glass they'd created. A week before that, he'd grabbed her by the throat, released her, and then lay facedown on the sofa holding a cushion over the back of his head, sobbing and moaning, lamenting what he'd done, apologizing to the upholstery. Once she'd caught her breath, she sat on the edge of the couch beside him, stroking his back like he was a cat. He couldn't see her face, hardened and numb.

Eventually, inevitably, Neil was sent home early on a slow night at the bar. From the sound of the key in the lock, she probably had time to shove everything back in the shoebox and tuck it under the table, but she was slow to react, her hands continuing to polish the freshly assembled gun with a rag. Her body again knowing before her mind: she wanted him to see.

For once, Neil was speechless. She felt his presence over her shoulder and continued rubbing the barrel for much longer than necessary. She waited for him to speak, to react to this tableau. Martha, in the kitchen, with the handgun.

Would he speak first, or would she turn around first? How did he read this scene, as her threatening his life or her own? She held the gun up to the dim pendant light, admiring its dull sheen. Nothing else in the apartment was this clean. In four and a half years, neither of them had ever dusted the bookshelves or the baseboards, or broken through the crust of toothpaste scum over the overflow drain. Their dark furniture grew implacably darker over the years, the air thickening like soup.

Whenever Martha went to look at job listings, she'd found herself clicking over to the housing ads instead, seduced by apartments that looked just like hers except empty. The bare floors licked by sunlight and sinks scrubbed angelic white, representing other lives. Sometimes she even emailed the agents and owners, though she never followed up. Pack and unpack. That morning, she'd seen a house mixed into her city's listings, despite its location in a town four hours away, and was startled by the low rent, similar to what she paid now for half of a one-bedroom but for the entirety of a furnished two-story Victorian. Three bedrooms and one bath, available immediately.

She saw herself sitting in the enclosed porch, the sky a fierce blue through the glass roof, greenhouse warm in all seasons.

Having nothing else to do, she put the gun back in the box, replaced the brushes, bottle, aerosol can, clean wipes, shook out the rag and folded it in quarters. She put the lid on the box and carried it as she stood from the table. She turned and looked past him, moving robotically. She walked straight to the bedroom. When she got to the closet, rather than putting the box back, she pulled out her suitcase—it had been a graduation gift from her father, old-fashioned in appearance and a beast in size, something a woman from an earlier time would bring on a transatlantic crossing. She put the gun at the bottom. There was a rushing sound in her ears, like passing trucks on a highway, urging her on: Move faster, before you lose your nerve. She'd need her computer and headset and mouse, her phone charger. She dumped in her hamper of dirty clothes, she ripped clothes from hangers, carried them in piles and armfuls, threw in whatever was at hand.

When she came out of the bedroom, dragging the suitcase behind her, Neil stood at the kitchen table, running his hand across the surface, as though the wood-patterned melamine could explain. He looked up and his mouth opened as she hurried past, stepped quickly into her boots, into the hallway, closed the door. She could hear him yank the door back open, the suitcase all but free-falling down the stairs behind her as she descended. She heard him call her name. Once, twice, three times. Astonished, then furious. Martha? Martha. Martha! The door to the outside and its finicky locks. He wasn't following, but she ran-walked down the sidewalk, as fast as she could move while tethered to the suitcase. Her legs pumping of their own volition, from an ancient instinct, her body finally victorious.

3.

Martha dreamed of June bugs crawling into her ear canals, up her nose. She dreamed they swam in the fluid that suspended her brain in her skull. Awake, she jerked her head from the pillow as a June bug traveled the outer coil of her upper ear, tender as a lover. She dreamed they moved under her skin, in her bloodstream, riding the current of her heartbeat like river rapids. Awake, she checked the thick arteries on the inside of her wrists—they would almost fit.

"Thank you for shopping with ShopGlobal. My name is Martha," she said, shaking beetles from the curtain into a trash can.

"Who am I speaking with?" she said, knocking beetles from the window.

"How can I help you?" she said, gathering their dazed, twitching forms from the windowsill.

"I can certainly help you with that," she said, scraping bugs from the lamp.

"I'm afraid there's nothing I can do," she said, scraping them from the desk.

"Is there anything else I can do for you today?" she said, scraping them from the bookshelves.

"Thank you for shopping with ShopGlobal. My name is Martha. Who am I speaking with?"

"Neil."

She paused. There were hundreds of ShopGlobal reps, once spread out over five call centers in five cities in three time zones, now in their own homes. He could call over and over for days on end and never reach her. "Hi, Neil. How can I help you?"

"I ordered a bottle of laundry detergent, and it was leaking when it arrived."

"I can definitely help you with that," she chirped. "Was the packaging damaged, or just the product itself?"

"Well, it soaked through the box, so I guess both." She and Neil, her Neil, had rarely spoken on the phone. This voice was huskier than she remembered his, with the sulky, dragged-out syllables of a teenager.

"I'm sorry to hear that. Would you like a refund or a replacement?"

"Replacement."

"No problem. Can you give me the order number?" She typed in the number he gave her, after brushing away a beetle that had fallen in the gap between the space bar and the row of keys above. "Hmm, that number isn't coming up for me. How long ago did you place the order?"

"About four months ago."

Martha's hand went to her stomach, which felt unsettled. She was certain she'd been eating the beetles, that she couldn't have noticed every single one to fall or crawl into her food. "And it just arrived?"

"No, it arrived four months ago."

"I'm sorry, but we only offer returns and replacements within sixty days."

"I didn't have time to call," he said. "I'm very busy."

"I am sorry," she repeated, "but that's the policy. There's nothing I can do."

"I paid for the detergent. And I just got a big soapy mess."

"I understand that."

"I'm very unhappy about this." His voice changed, as though he was suddenly fully awake, fully engaged in this conversation. "What did you say your name was again?"

"Martha."

"Do you like your job, Martha?"

She'd gotten this question from customers before. "It's a living."

"Are you happy? In general, with your life?"

"I suppose so, sir. Is there anything further I can help you with, regarding your order?"

"Where are you?"

She swiped at her neck, thinking she'd felt another bug, but there was nothing there. "I'm not sure that's relevant."

"I just want to know if you're in a call center in Bangladesh, faking an American accent."

"I am indeed in the continental US, sir."

"That's vague. What city?"

"Sir, if I can't help you with your order, it's time for us to say goodbye."

"Don't you dare hang up on me! Don't you fucking hang up on me!"

She was allowed to disconnect him as soon as he used the word "fucking," but it would trigger a review of her call logs. "Tell you what, Neil," she said, "how about I give you a coupon for free shipping and fifteen percent off your next order?"

"I want to know where you are. Tell me where you are, Martha."

She'd been hovering her cursor over the red disconnect button, but now her hand slipped from the mouse and onto the desk. "Neil?" she whispered.

"Yes? What?"

"Is that you?"

"What do you mean? Yes, it's Neil, I'm still here. Did you hang up on me?"

"I can't help you." She was still whispering. She couldn't hang up on him now. She didn't want anyone ever listening to the recording. "I wish things were different. I wish things hadn't happened the way they did. But I can't help you."

Silence. They listened to each other breathe. The stranger on the other end sighed and said, finally, "I'll take the coupon."

November. The sun rose late and in a rush, barreling westward to an early bedtime. The windows of Martha's rented house fogged like a sauna. The weatherman predicted the driest winter in twenty years, insufficient snowmelt in the spring to fill the reservoirs. "I hope I'm wrong," he said.

When the doorbell rang in the evening, Martha didn't recognize the sound. She hadn't used the front door in weeks. From the outside, at a distance, the window in the mudroom door had looked blacked out, as though taped over from the inside. Up close, it resolved into the densely packed insects. She opened the internal door and expected a tsunami of June bugs, an ecstatic wave that might carry her back into the living room.

The unlit mudroom seemed almost colder than outside, a refrigerated chill. And it was quiet—the buzz of wings that flexed and closed but never lifted off had been reduced from a belting choir to the distinct notes of individual June bugs, each with their own rhythm. A person stood there in the dark, chin tucked to chest. Inside the mudroom, already past the outer door and its faulty latch. He lifted his head, and something in the motion was familiar. Her eyes adjusted, light spilling from the house behind her. The walls looked smooth as they hadn't since her first week. The floor was thickly carpeted with husks, beetles dead long enough to mummify, sucked clean of anything soft or wet. The killing winter that Barb had promised had finally come.

"Neil," she said.

"Can I come in?" he asked.

She held the door for him, and immediately felt it as a strike against her somewhere, heard facts read aloud in an imagined court: She invited him in. She held open the door.

They stood together in the entryway, on the cheery red-and-white carpet runner. He was wearing a denim jacket she didn't recognize, two or three sizes too big, the same light wash as his jeans, both smeared with grease. He worried the edges of the pockets with his fingers. His knuckles and the tip of his nose were red and raw, like he'd been out in the cold for a long time. He looked boyish and lost, and despite herself, she felt the urge to run him a bath, cook him a hot meal, tuck him into bed.

"Nice place," he said.

She didn't reply.

"It's so good to see you," Neil said. He reached for her. She took a step back. He let his arms drop. "I've missed you so much. I was so worried. It was like you vanished off the face of the earth."

And yet he'd found her. She could imagine a few ways: through the bank, through her work, some charmed employee giving up Martha's new address. Neil made a lot in tips at the bar, despite his total disdain for the patrons. She'd always wondered how he could turn it on and off.

"Can we sit down and talk?" He looked past her, through the archway to the kitchen, partially blocked by the jutting refrigerator. "Maybe in there?"

He seated himself at the breakfast table. Martha trailed behind him and leaned in the doorway, her wide frame filling it, her arms crossed. "Come sit with me," he said.

Her eyes flicked toward the top of the fridge.

"Martha?"

She couldn't stop staring at the shoebox, within easy reach on the three-quarter-size refrigerator.

Neil noticed. He stood and followed the direction of her gaze, as she stayed still, paralyzed. Dead June bugs tumbled down the face of the fridge as he pulled the shoebox forward. He opened it and removed the gun. He held it laid across his open palms, as a priest holds a Bible during a liturgy, as a child holds an injured baby bird, and carried it back to the table. He sat in the farthest seat, the gun on the table before him. Sitting in imitation of her the day she left.

"I don't like guns," Neil said, softly. "You know that. I don't even like guns in movies. You can't focus on anything else when there's a gun in a scene. They change things too fast. The bad guys just fall away. There's no buildup. No conversation. No intimacy."

"You prefer an intimate killing."

"I prefer," he said, "when the bad guy has time to think. To apologize."

"Are you apologizing?"

"Am *I* apologizing?" Neil flushed. "You brought a gun into our home!"

She remembered the first time, how she'd kept coming back to that night and thinking: I shoved him first.

"And then you just left. You left without saying goodbye or telling me where you were going. You left without telling me why. You left without talking. Without giving me a chance to talk."

Her gaze kept darting away from Neil's face, drawn to flickers of motion. To the June bugs on the ceiling, stumbling to their doom in the chandelier. The June bugs on the floor. June bugs lining the baseboards. June bugs in the coffeepot. June bugs climbing out of the drawers and cabinets. June bugs in the swirl of the stove elements. Only a few on the breakfast table, crawling in slow circles around the gun. She could tell her inattention was making him angrier.

"Tell me why you left," he said.

There was no answer she hadn't given before, that he hadn't argued away. "Because I wanted to."

"That's not an answer!"

"Because I don't love you anymore."

He let out a small, pained cry. He jumped to his feet and picked up the gun in one hand, in one swing, with a steadiness and confidence she'd never possessed. He pointed it at her. "Why? Why don't you love me anymore?"

"It's not loaded," she said. She wasn't sure. She had a distinct memory of releasing the magazine, pulling the slide back to eject the chambered cartridge, emptying the magazine of the remaining five rounds, reinserting it. But was that the last time she'd cleaned the gun, or some time before? The nights blurred together. How could she be sure of anything she did at three in the morning, wandering downstairs out of a beetle nightmare, swiping the bugs from her nightshirt, combing them from her hair?

He waved the gun around, the muzzle pointing in all directions before landing back on her, watching as she flinched. "It feels loaded. It feels heavy." His voice was shrill.

She remembered the chicken restaurant where the bus had dropped her off and Mrs. Cutler had picked her up. She could almost smell it. She wished that she'd gone inside, sunk into a booth, ordered a plate. Sat a little longer at that way station between two lives, where she could have done anything, gone anywhere, been anything.

"Tell me why. Tell me why you don't love me. Tell me why I'm not lovable. Tell me what's so wrong with me." His pointer finger slipped inside the trigger guard. Her vision tunneled to just the barrel of the gun, everything else blurring, falling away.

A June bug emerged from the muzzle, poking out of the hole like a groundhog. In the intensity of her focus, she could see even the craggy texture of its filament legs, its chestnut-shaped abdomen. It crawled up over the top of the gun. A second followed, a third. They poured out of the barrel, as filled with them as every other container and crevice in the house; she must have left the shoebox lid askew. They skittered in their aimless way across the slide and the guard and the grip and Neil's hand, into the sleeve of his jacket. He dropped the gun and stumbled backward, into the table, knocking his head on the low, swinging light fixture. June bugs cascaded out of the chandelier, dropping on his head and shoulders, tumbling slowly through the air. She'd never gotten around to cleaning it out. He screamed, batting them away as their legs scrambled for purchase on his face, as they slipped and fell down the collar of his shirt. The table had struck the wall, dislodging yet more bugs, frenzied as they hit the floor.

Neil fell onto his back—still swatting at his face and neck, smearing pops of blood where he'd crushed them, scratching at his clothes—belly-up and helpless, posed as she often found the beetles. She thought of all the things she could say, that Barb had said to her, when she asked why it was only her house, what she'd done to deserve this: They don't sting, they don't bite. They're harmless. They'll go away. Many of them, in fact, were already dead, curled up, desiccated little bodies that had fallen into Neil's shrieking mouth, and the rest would soon follow. She said nothing. She thought of the task ahead, through the winter. She'd have to sweep out the old porch, the mausoleum the bugs had made of her sunroom and mudroom, filling trash bags with the husks, squishing stragglers as she went. She could leave the bags on Barb's doorstep, as proof it had happened. Or she could empty them out onto the front lawn, a mound of conquered insects, a warning to anyone who might pass.

BRIDEZILLA

The first reports of the sea monster were broadcast the day Arthur proposed to Leah. News outlets put "sea monster" in quotation marks in headlines and chyrons, usually followed by a question mark.

Arthur and Leah were eating breakfast in a diner. CNN played on a TV on a high corner shelf, facing Leah. The most popular footage of the monster, taken on a phone by a commercial fisherman off the coast of Hawaii, had already played twice over the course of their meal. Technically, it was an amalgamation of brainless multicellular organisms—chemically linked, lurching as one. Yes, it was easy to confuse the thick, bonded chains for tentacular limbs, the greater central mass for a body, to imagine its twitching-nerve reactions as movement coordinated by a central mind, but the science assured otherwise. Yes, videos of it surfacing and splashing down like a whale—a slimy, eyeless, mottled neon orange and yellow whale—were alarming, but as far as anyone could tell, it was a harmless cannibal, consuming only the type of microscopic sea life of which it was composed. Digesting some, enveloping others. How does it choose, Leah wondered. How does it choose whether you get eaten or you join?

"We should get married," Arthur said, mouth full of pancakes. Leah put down her fork. "Why?"

"Because you want to," he said.

"Oh, do I? And you don't?"

"I don't care either way. And if one of us really wants to do something, and the other is indifferent, we should do it." He cut and speared another cross-section of his short stack. "Like if I really wanted pizza for dinner, and you were fine with anything, we would get pizza."

"I'm not sure I want to get married if you think marriage is comparable to pizza."

"Pizza is one of the great wonders of the universe," Arthur replied, gravely. "And I want to be with you for the rest of our lives. It's the bureaucracy that I'm indifferent to."

"I feel unconvinced."

"I'm not going to argue for it," he said. "I just want you to know that if a wedding is something you want, I'm game."

Leah stared past Arthur's head, where the shaky video of the monster was playing for a third time. On-screen, a living island of sludge in vibrant, toxic colors rose from the sea. "How romantic," she said.

Leah knew her friends despised weddings. Marriage was an archaic, unnecessary, patriarchal institution. They thought of themselves as free-love bohemians, despite having all ended up in monogamous, long-term, two-person partnerships, despite mostly working in corporate jobs and at universities. They thought weddings showed hubris, or cast a jinx, or were a desperate attempt to save a relationship that everyone knew was already failing. They thought this despite some of them actually *being married*: two married at city hall over a weekend without telling anyone, announcing it on Facebook on Monday morning, and another couple married in the garden of their ground-floor apartment with only their immediate families present. But each time a sibling or cousin or friend from college tied the knot, they crowed with horror over brunch: the wasted money, the gendered rituals, drunken toasts, hideous dresses, photo slideshows, adult women holding parasols, tiers of cupcakes. They would announce they had to go to a wedding or, worse yet, an engagement party, bridal shower, or bachelor/bachelorette party, with a gagging gesture, a kill-me throat-slash. "White people!" they'd laugh, despite—or because, Leah was never sure—the whole group being white themselves.

Leah looked in the windows of bridal stores, the mannequins invariably headless, golems for self-insertion. She was tall, lean, and blond, and it was easy to blur her reflection on the surface of the glass into the sweeping, regal dresses behind it. She felt drawn to the displays, repulsed by them, a magnet of changing poles. Weddings were obscene in any era, but especially in this one, a narcissistic spectacle at the end of the world.

Arthur listened to her change her mind every other day in his genial, even-keeled way, and continued to express no opinion. "If you want a wedding, let's have a wedding," he said. "If you don't want a wedding, we don't have to have one." He was physically large, slow-moving, agreeable—a steady, mountain-like man. Her friends said they loved Arthur, they adored him, but they treated him like a piece of furniture or, at best, a beloved pet she brought everywhere. Everyone agreed he was good for her, a stabilizing force.

Leah had large blue eyes and an upturned nose. In her teens and twenties, she'd often been told she should have been a model or an actress. She'd never had any aspirations in these areas, but she still noted that people had stopped suggesting it. Her parents had been comfortably, upward-trending middle class, and were aging independently and without fuss. She'd gotten good grades and had been well-liked in school. She was lucky enough to share a co-op apartment with Arthur, while their friends moved farther and farther out into the suburbs. She had a coveted job writing reports and newsletters for a nonprofit with an absentminded billionaire's wife at the top. She volunteered at her neighborhood food bank on the weekend, portioning dry goods from large sacks into small bags.

She had once liked pretty things, the most basic of pretty things, the lingua franca of femininity: candles, mirrors, flowers, pastel colors. She'd once wanted to get married in a big white dress on a beach at sunset. She'd wanted four children and enough bedrooms to house them all. She wasn't sure when that had changed, why all these things now struck her as grotesque and fetishistic. She felt conscious of an army of twenty-two-year-olds at her back, with infinitely more energy and talent, who wouldn't hesitate to kill for her apartment or job.

When Leah asked Arthur if he wanted children, he said, "I don't know. Do you?"

"Do you think it's immoral to have children now?"

"Yeah, maybe."

But also: the sweet soft smell of an infant's head, a toddler's astonished shrieking laugh as their fingers grasped at the newness of anything, everything.

The day after the sea monster appeared on the other side of the world, four people were gunned down in a grocery store downtown. Three days later, a crane fell from a construction site during a windstorm and crushed two cars, and an embezzlement scandal involving three city council members came to light. This, of course, was only the local news.

"So let's get married on a beach at sunset," Arthur said.

"We can't."

"Why?"

Because they kept their windows closed all summer to keep out the wildfire smoke, the sun a defined red disk in the haze that gave everything a Martian glow. Because the waterfront homes in their city that used to be rented as wedding venues were being abandoned as uninsurable, prone to flooding, poised on eroding cliffsides. Because the ocean was now a noxious, primordial soup, spitting up monsters.

In a thrift store, on a rack of nightgowns, Leah found the dress: a white full-length slip, the hem just past her ankles, that fell straight down and made her look like a sliver of moonlight. She kept it in the back of her closet for months and told no one.

The monster created sound waves that confused the echolocation of other sea life, sent them chasing after imaginary prey. Scientists were quoted explaining that the synchronized vibrational movement of millions of tiny creatures was not "talking" or "singing," as some reports had it—the conglomeration contained no structures capable of even rudimentary communication. The monster had first been pushed northwest, toward Japan, and was now rounding southwest again on the global currents, on an arc that bent toward Alaska and eventually California, projected to circle the Pacific Ocean indefinitely. It was still growing, but the latest science suggested that the nature of the bonds holding it together limited how large the monster could grow before breaking apart, crushed under its own weight. The world resigned to its existence, and it rarely made the news. Someone made an app that pinned the locations of confirmed sightings and projected the monster's path, such that Leah could take out her phone and see approximately where it was in the world at any given moment.

Arthur found the harbor cruise. "It's not the beach," he said, "but it's on the water." The all-in-one package was three hours and up to twenty-five guests. If the weather was good, they'd be married on the deck by the captain, who was ordained by the Universal Life Church. Their guests would be served the dinner cruise dinner, choice of steak or pasta. The crew member who usually took group photos before boarding, hustling parties in front of a life-size backdrop of the very dock they stood on— except consistently lit, forever sunny, with the cruise company logo in the corner—would be their wedding photographer.

No fuss, no muss. *Painless* was the word that came to mind. Leah felt crushed by disappointment just looking at the website. "It's perfect," she said.

In the women's washroom, which served as Leah's bridal suite, she could feel the vibration of the boat's engine when she leaned against the wall. The ocean had been visibly choppy that afternoon, and her stomach swayed along with the docked boat. She took yogic breaths. A potent mix of smells—sea, shit, diesel, hand soap—accompanied each inhale.

She longed for a full-length mirror. She looked ghastly in the strip mirror above the sinks. The woman she'd hired to do her hair and makeup had already left, so there was nothing to be done about the sharp borders between garish patches of color on her face. The pink eye shadow that had looked feminine and rosy on their trial day now looked like conjunctivitis, and the foundation was so thick and ill matched that her face seemed to hover in front of her head, like a mask made from a paper plate.

Leah's mother fussed with the hem of her dress. "I just cannot get it to lie flat," she said. "It keeps wrinkling."

"Mom, just leave it."

"You want it to look good in the pictures. Those pictures are forever."

Unable to see herself below the shoulders, Leah fiddled with the too-long straps that made the neckline sit slack and precariously low across her chest, the bodice cupping her upper rib cage instead of her breasts. It occurred to her only now that the slip had probably been someone's bridal lingerie, probably someone dead. She pictured their adult child emptying whole drawers into garbage bags. The dress had been so delicate she'd been afraid to wash it, and a musty smell lingered. Most likely, both bride and groom were dead now, the ghost of their wedding night consummation sunken into the fibers, along with whatever joy or pain it had heralded.

She batted her mother's hands away from her own butt. "Mom, why don't you go back out and greet people as they board?"

"I told you that you needed ushers. Everything is so disorganized."

Because of the intermittent rain, the ceremony would be on the karaoke stage, hastily decorated in crepe paper streamers like a middle-school dance. The steaks were turning to leather under the galley heat lamps, the pasta congealing to a candy-red sludge.

"I want to talk to Arthur," Leah said.

"You're not supposed to see each other. Bad luck and all that."

"I know, but—but he doesn't care about that stuff."

"He doesn't care much about anything."

"Mom." Leah's hands were cold and bloodless. She flexed her fingers. Her seasickness was worsening. "I need to get some air."

"You're just going to go out there? Before the ceremony?"

"Sure, why not?"

"Because you're supposed to make an entrance," her mother said. "Also, the rain will ruin your makeup."

Too late for that, she thought. "I'll be quick."

As soon as she ducked out the restroom door, she saw that nearly everyone had gathered on the outside upper deck to take pictures of the city skyline, about to recede and widen behind them as the boat left dock. The rain had just stopped, the sun peeking through a tear in the quilted gray sky. Only Leah's uncle Sven and Arthur's youngest sister, Jenny, remained inside, talking near the base of the stairs. Sven had his hand on the wall above Jenny's head, Jenny being sixteen and almost a full foot shorter than him, his body tented over hers.

She saw her friends' backs through the windows, their craning arms, phones lifted like offerings. They were laughing at something. Her, surely. Despite her efforts to keep everything casual and low-key, she still felt silly, nakedly hungry for attention, like a child in a cardboard birthday crown. She saw Arthur in his rented tuxedo, the pants too short and the jacket straining against the bulk of his upper body. The man she loved, the last man she would ever love. The hunch of his back, the shape of diminished dreams. Ungenerous thoughts pressed against the back of her eyes.

Rather than brave the crowd, Leah went out the door they'd boarded through, which led to the enclosed side deck. She immediately felt better. The air was damp and cold, June dressed as February.

A crewman worked to detach the gangway. He was handsome, she thought, dark with close-cropped hair, attractive even in a neon visibility vest and navy coveralls. The sight of the only exit closing, the only connection to land being severed, sent a bolt of panic through her limbs.

Her muscles suddenly taut and primed, she ran down the ramp in her sandals, their flat bottoms slick against the wet rubber. The crewman hardly looked up as she flashed by. Something dawned slowly in his face as he tossed the ropes to the other crew member on the dock, as the ramp raised and tucked neatly into its horizontal resting place, as a triumphant horn blasted over the roar of the engines, the gap between the dock and the boat widening, at first only by inches.

Leah stood on the other side.

They stared at each other. She could read his lips, clear as day: *Oh shit.*

He leaned over the railing as the boat continued to drift away. He tilted his head and gestured toward the door with his chin. Something like: Did you mean to do that? Should I get them to stop this thing?

She raised a finger to her lips. *Shh.*

She could tell by his eyes and the shape of his mouth that he was laughing.

The crewman on the dock gaped at her. "Oh shit," he echoed. He was handsome too, in a different way—scruffy and windburned, long hair tucked against his neck by a gray ski hat.

The boat's path would curve right as it left the harbor and soon all the guests would see her from the rear deck, shivering on land in her nightgown-dress. Some part of her believed she could avoid disaster if she just stayed out of sight.

She ran along the boardwalk and ducked down the first set of stairs she came across, which led down to the water. The small beach had always been unpopular because of the reek of the water treatment output pipe and, more recently, the added smell of rotting seaweed and shellfish.

The only person on the rocky sand played with his dog near the sign that indicated dogs were forbidden on city beaches. He threw a ball and his shorthaired mutt launched itself into the frigid Pacific to retrieve it over and over. The water was a strange color, swamp green with a reddish tint at the horizon line.

The rain began again, a light touch dotting her dress, deflating Leah's absurd, puffed-up hair. The man with the dog glanced back at her between throws. The wind blew out her skirt like a sail, and she felt like an apparition come to haunt him, a flickering white flame rising up from the sand. She felt her makeup starting to run down her face like the shift before a landslide, a plane of solid ground liquefying.

"Oh shit," she said aloud.

Until this moment, her mind had jumped ahead to returning to their apartment, hopping in a hot shower, baking a frozen pizza. Like Arthur would be there, as he always had. Her sweet, dependable Arthur, who never complained about anything. Like she'd be able to explain it to him—*they were raising the gangway and I just felt—I had to—everything was so ugly and wrong—*

Even Arthur couldn't forgive the humiliation of the boat entering the bay with no bride. The confusion of the guests. Searching the ship for her, thinking there was nowhere for her to have gone. Her mother, smug and unsurprised. Would they think she fell overboard? Tipped over the railing in a fit of nerves and champagne? When would the laughing crewman reveal what he'd seen? How difficult was it to turn around that slow, wide vessel?

The dog was oblivious to Leah, the rain, his owner's growing discomfort, and even the terrible, seductive smells of the beach. His world consisted entirely of the ball, its high arc through the sky, tiny splash, buoyant resurfacing. He returned the ball to his owner without enticement, and the man had a good throwing arm, pitching it fast and far each time.

Eventually, the owner called, "Okay, Hammy, time to go," and the dog stopped abruptly, some distance away, ball in mouth. After a moment of contemplation, Hammy trotted over to Leah. He sniffed her exposed feet, then lifted his nose from her calves to her crotch, streaking filth from his snout along the white skirt.

"Hello," she murmured. She reached to pet him. He pressed his body against her legs through the long skirt, his wagging tail throwing seawater into her face. The ball forced his mouth into the shape of a clown's painted smile.

"Hammy!" The owner ran toward them.

She squatted down. Hammy jumped up in response, clumps of wet sand falling down the front of her dress. She embraced him, and he submitted, his chaotic energy bound in her arms, his whole back half swinging metronomically.

The owner had reached them. "I'm so sorry," he said.

She could tell, from his hesitancy, that she looked like a madwoman in her soaked dress and sloughed-off makeup. She smiled down at the distinct pawprints Hammy had left among the continents of mud and dirt.

"Your dress is ruined," he said, his tone accusatory.

"It was already ruined," she said. As she released the dog, he spat the ball directly into her hands, which cupped to catch it.

She reared back and threw. She was surprised at her own power, how long the ball seemed to be airborne, its long trajectory over the ocean. In the thickening rain, the wind picking up and tossing grit in her eyes, she couldn't quite make out where it hit the water. The dog barreled back into the ocean. They watched him swim, his floppy-eared head shrinking with distance.

"Hammy, that's too far," the owner called. "Hammy! Come back now! Hammy, come! Come, Hammy!"

Leah could just make out the dog's muzzle, pointed upward, turn back toward them. The rain fell harder.

The dog's head disappeared under the opaque water.

The two of them ran toward the ocean. The man was faster, Leah's stride constricted by her long, drenched skirt. He stopped at the shoreline. Leah kicked off her sandals. The too-long straps slipped easily off her shoulders. She stepped out of the puddle of dress at her feet.

Waves knocked her to her knees as she waded in. She hadn't swum in the ocean since she was a child. As she found her stroke, the water seemed more resistant than she remembered, her body more buoyant, like swimming in gelatin. The rotten-fish-and-gasoline smell that had been embedded in her sinuses since the harbor cruise now flooded her brain. When she opened her eyes under the water, they burned. She could see nothing.

The soupy water forced her to the surface, bursting through clots of seaweed. She felt the stringy plant life draping her shoulders, clinging to her treading limbs. She couldn't see the dog anywhere.

She'd thrown the ball.

She'd abandoned Arthur at the altar.

The beach and the figure of the dog's owner seemed impossibly far, much farther away than she could have swum in that time. Yet her toes grazed solid ground. She could stand, between being thrown off her feet by the current. But even as she stood, she saw the shoreline vanishing, the abyss of ocean growing between her and the city.

She tried to make sense of what she was seeing, her eyes still stinging. Through the dark murk, she didn't seem to be standing on the ocean's bottom but on a moving, shifting surface, propelling farther out to sea. A warm current swirled around her, like a hot water tap streaming into a cold bath. She struggled against the seaweed still wrapped around her arms and neck and waist, dangling from her ankles. She tried to swipe the seawater from her eyes.

The seaweed was neon orange.

She twisted around, entangling herself further. She finally spotted a furry blotch floating on a patch of neon yellow slime, under a lattice of slick, luminescent yellow ribbons. Hammy.

She felt herself trembling, her skin prickling, her heart shaking out of rhythm. Her whole body was vibrating, resonating like a struck string. She thought of Arthur. She pictured him at the tuxedo-rental shop, squeezed into the too-small suit, not wanting to contradict the salesperson, not wanting to trouble them, wanting to make them happy. The way he always wanted to make Leah happy.

The orange and yellow slime gathered to her, suckered to her flesh, pulled her apart. The image of Arthur slipped away. The approval of her friends, what she wanted, what she told herself she didn't want. Her everlasting importance. She understood, for just a breath, the ecosystem of her body, all the creatures she housed on her skin, in her hair, in her intestines, all her wants and dreams and loves as stimulus and meat, fragile and dependent on every other life. She readied herself to join an ancient, unstoppable mind.

DO YOU REMEMBER CANDY

A small number of people would remember a release in their sinuses, as with a sudden change in altitude. Fewer still had a day or two when everything tasted a little different, like the aftereffect of Sichuan peppercorns or miracle fruit. For Allie, as for most people, it happened all at once.

It happens in her neighborhood café, where she's gone to escape the mundane chaos of any, every morning: halfway to her daughter's school, Jay announces she's forgotten her homework. They argue over whether it's better to be on time without the homework (Allie's opinion) or to be late with the homework (Jay's opinion, but they wouldn't *be* late if Allie would just stop talking and turn the car around). She drops Jay off, drives home, retrieves the homework, drives back, explains the situation to the school office—where visitors must check in, even parents popping in to jam a folder into their fifth grader's locker, and why do fifth graders already have lockers, what happened to cubbies, and why is the inside of Jay's locker sticky to the touch—and drives home a second time. She settles in front of the computer, where she's greeted by nineteen separate emails from one client, working through tweaks they want—or maybe don't want, or maybe want something along those lines, oh, they'll leave it up to her, really—on the website mock-up she sent the day before.

She heads to a café, where she can work at a table from which she can't see last night's dishes. She orders a cappuccino and a chocolate croissant at the register. She imagines sinking her teeth into butter and foam, even as she reminds herself croissants are six for four dollars at the grocery store and instant coffee is pennies per cup—

She sits outside. She's the only one on the patio, as the morning is cool. She stirs a sugar cube into her coffee, enjoying the ritual of the tiny spoon that serves no other purpose, the way it rings against the rim of the cup. She sips.

Her cappuccino tastes very faintly metallic, mineral, like sucking on a rock. Like stale air. Hot water from a kettle that needs descaling.

It tastes like nothing.

She spits out her first bite of the croissant, sputtering. She must have eaten a piece of the wrapper. She wipes the flakes of pastry from her tongue; they feel and taste like shreds of paper. She picks up the croissant and turns it over, inspecting it on all sides. There's no wrapper.

She bites into it a second time. The melted chocolate wraps her tongue with a mucous film that tastes of her own breath, like nasal drip from a cold. She spits into her napkin again.

She picks up her dishes and goes inside to complain, only to discover a line of people doing the same, holding plates of pastries and sandwiches with one bite missing, near-full cups and glasses. The barista is in tears, on the phone with the manager. It's not their fault, Allie thinks. Her stomach grumbles. She chugs her watery, flavorless coffee and puts her uneaten croissant in the bus bin.

The Vietnamese restaurant next door has just opened. The scent of the broth, beefy and herbaceous, usually pulls her in from the street. Today, as she enters, she can smell only industrial floor cleaner, and a smell that reminds her of Jay's old day care—dirty shoes, felted carpet, sweaty children.

Her first mouthful of noodles tastes like boiled plastic, water from a disposable bottle left in a hot car, the chewed end of a drinking straw. She again spits reflexively, turning her head as though sneezing. A wad of rice starch and saliva splatters on the floor by her shoe. The waitress rushes in her direction just as a man on the other side of the restaurant, the only other patron, spits a bolus of spring roll back onto his plate.

That afternoon, she goes through her fridge and pantry shelf by shelf, frantic and disbelieving. The cheese tastes like putty, flour paste. The bread is dry as cotton batting. An apple is like crunching on ice. The deli meat as plainly inedible as slivers of rubber. The heatless pain of the mustard, like biting the inside of her mouth.

The stock markets crash, multibillion-dollar industries collapse, but so much doesn't change. It dominates the news, but only briefly. Allie isn't released from her obligations. Jay's school still sends home newsletters and demands and assigns too much homework. Clients still expect their designs on time.

Their emails acknowledge nothing; they hope she's well, they send their best. There are only a few weeks where Allie feels the world grieve with her, where airports, bus depots, and train stations are slammed and ticket prices skyrocket. People like Allie trying to go home, to taste their grandmother's father's sister's best friend's chocolate barbecued kimchi parathas pumpkin pie stew, one last time. They shovel flavorless ash into their mouths.

She hadn't known, until it happened, that she was one kind of person and there even was another, could never have dreamed that seemingly everyone she knew would adapt so quickly. At pickup, the other mothers confess to feeling freed from the endless cycle of meal planning, shopping, cooking, dishes. Freed, in some cases, from food's push-pull addiction, the accusatory cult of thinness. The search for a cause, for a cure, loses steam and funding over the first couple of years— the absence of physical explanation leads to spiritual ones, psychological ones, conspiracy theories, and then, finally, to a collective shrug. As with so much else, as with whole buildings that vanish and get paved over and no one remembers quite what was there before, this is just how it is.

Of course there are other joys. Or so Allie tells herself. There's Jay, a creature of such beauty and independence and unrecognizable desires that Allie can hardly believe they share a home, much less that she'd given her life. Like living with a gazelle, seeing it leap across a doorway out of the corner of your eye— all skinny-legged, alien grace. Jay seems remarkably *busy* for a ten-year-old, eleven-year-old, twelve. Always in a hurry, in the middle of a project or invented game. She mostly asks Allie where things are: Mom, do we have any glue? Mom, can I cut up this T-shirt?

Jay takes her vitamins and swallows her boiled porridge of grains and slimy greens. She's already learned to bypass her mouth like a bird. Allie often forgets. Her mouth chews, stubborn and mournful. Jay leaps from her chair, eager to return to whatever she's been doing. Allie touches her wrist to stop her. Jay's hands are already approaching the size of her own. She will be tall, almost certainly taller than Allie. Adolescent Jay obliterated infant Jay like a parasite bursting from its host.

"Do you remember candy?" Allie asks.

"Yeah."

"Do you miss it?"

"I guess."

"What was your favorite?"

"I don't know." Jay strains in the direction of her bedroom. Sometimes, when Allie talks to her daughter, it feels like approaching a famous person at a party. Feeling desperate to impress as they stare past her, scan the crowd for someone more important. She lets her go.

Jay walks in on her mother curled up in the empty bathtub, fully clothed in the dark. Allie is elbow-deep in an enormous jar of cheese puffs, her face stained neon orange. Jay would have found this unsettling even in the days before the puffs tasted like packing peanuts.

Jay's friend invites Jay and Allie—a steadfast atheist of Presbyterian extraction—to Shabbos dinner. Jay wears her red velour skater dress, carefully arranges her bangs. As her friend's mother sings softly over the candles and dishes in the dim room, Allie starts sobbing, wiping snot from her face with one of their host's good cloth napkins. Jay is humiliated. It's like crying at the funeral of someone you didn't know. She fumes silently through the whole ride home, but her mother doesn't even notice.

Allie emails her friend Fiona. Fiona had also been a freelancer when they met, and their friendship had consisted of going out for lunch or late breakfast in the middle of a weekday, marveling at the fact that they could, but now Fiona is back at a full-time office job. Allie finds herself typing, "Do you remember candy?" She wants to ask people this all the time. Do they really remember food, not just that it had existed, but the sensations of it? Can they still conjure it up in their minds, make the juices in their mouths run?

She and Fiona used to go out for dim sum together. Does Fiona remember steamed char siu bao? Tearing one in half, releasing a whisper of steam. The bao like a fluffy, sun-warmed towel wrapped around your shoulders after you emerged from a cold lake, sucking the cold from your bare limbs and dripping swimsuit. The sticky pork, its caramelized glaze, the note of ferment and dark soy as the meat shredded, drawing out the sweetness in the bun. Allie writes more than she intended. The words run together, breathless and confiding.

Do you remember? Does anyone remember?

Fiona answers within the day. *I showed your email to my whole office. We remember.* And then an email from someone Allie doesn't know: *Hi, I work with Fiona. Can you do a soft-poached egg?*

Allie thinks about soft-poached eggs, on and off, for the rest of the week. The dim sum email came to her in a flood of sorrow, a fugue state of inspiration, but she considers the egg the way she conceptualizes a design for work. Or, more accurately, the way she conceptualized designs when she was in school, and the pairing of colors and typefaces, materials and objects from different historical or aesthetic movements, still thrilled her. She invites Fiona's coworker to her house. She asks him to come in the early afternoon, before Jay gets home from school.

He leaves work and tells no one. She hurries him inside. It would look like an affair to the neighbors—he stands on her doorstep at an illicit, stolen time of day, in the brazenness of sunlight, his face raw with want. She closes the thin curtains in the living room, muddying the bright afternoon.

She has him lie on his back on the floor. The room is just this side of too warm. She has painted a swatch of rich, saturated orange on a piece of card stock, suggestive of an egg yolk but with more pink undertones. She then mounted the card across the head of a flexible-neck desk lamp, which she now bends so the card hovers over his eyes, casting the faintest orange reflection on his skin. She found a pair of elbow-length evening gloves made of silk jersey at a thrift store; she lifted them from the accessories rack and knew by feel that they were the right ones.

She coats his hands and arms with a silicone lube that she knows, from experience, sits slickly on top of the skin and never seems to absorb, even hours later in the shower. She puts the gloves on for him, settles each finger carefully in place.

She kneels to the side of him, where she can reach him, but he can't see her without turning his head. She scrapes a butter knife against a plate near his ear (in the future, she'll omit this, thinking it corny, amateurish), and in one smooth, fluid gesture, she pulls off the gloves. The motion of the silk across his skin, and that warm, creamy orange that fills his field of vision, sends a shiver up his arm and into his chest, where the sensation drips slowly from his ribs.

In the early days, he went back to the diner where he'd eaten his last egg. He sat in the same booth, ordered it the same way, sprinkled it with salt, every detail the same. He slit into the egg with the side of a fork and put it in his mouth. It quivered and flopped down his throat like a goldfish.

Lying on Allie's floor, he can't taste it, but the melancholy of not-tasting it is nearer, sweeter, than that day at the diner: the patched vinyl booth and the checkered floor and the speckled off-white plate and the hard angles of the saltshaker, the horror of what an actual egg had become. Similar to the way, after his last breakup, he almost enjoyed wallowing, playing sad music and revisiting dusky memories and feeling justified in mistreating other women, but the pain of actually seeing his ex was too bright, too sharp, too cutting.

When he offers to pay Allie, she doesn't refuse. He puts a twenty-dollar bill on her desk. Later, this, too, will strike her as insulting. At her height, Allie will charge a thousand dollars per session.

The next request, from another of Fiona's coworkers, is a slightly underripe pear. That's how I used to like them, the woman explains. Allie sands and polishes an already-smooth wooden dowel. On her way to pick up Jay from school, she drives past a landscaping crew pruning back some bushes and trees that edge a yard. The branches are gnarled and unruly, some of the cuttings six feet long, but the individual leaves are dime-sized and delicate. She convinces the crew to let her take the whole pile, shoving the plant matter into her hatchback trunk.

"What are those for?" Jay asks.

Distractedly, Allie replies, "A work project."

Over several days, Allie builds a rounded lean-to structure from the greenery in her office, like an igloo made of plants, a tunnel running through the middle that would fit a person crawling or lying down. She works with a pair of hedge trimmers, with twine and zip ties and carpenter's glue. She has a box light pointing directly over the structure, so the light is visible from inside, filtered through the leaves. She plays with different color filters, that one too cool, that one too yellow.

Her second client arrives with the same furtive air as the first. When Allie answers the door, the woman looks nervous, fidgety. Almost ashamed. It feels like a weakness, a deficiency of character, to be pining for the past this way. The strip of fast-food restaurants near their highway exit is a one-road ghost town, buildings emptied of everything not bolted down, windows molding over. Abandoned livestock wander the roads of farming communities. There were early, hopeful articles about turning the tide on climate change, but how resilient the machine turned out to be: how quickly there were new businesses selling new products, or old products remarketed, with a new pipeline behind them. How quickly there were inoffensive nutritional gels and drinks, new vices, old vices reengineered and soaring in popularity, workers reabsorbed at a disadvantage.

In Allie's office, the woman shimmies into the miniature plant house, feet-first. Allie hands her the slippery, silken wooden dowel, now coated with menthol oil that sucks the heat from her fingers. Allie reaches inside and briefly feels for the contours of the woman's features, then lays a cool, wet cloth over her face. Allie had experimented with different exotic fabrics but found the slightly rough, cheap dishcloths she already had in her kitchen worked best. She counts to thirty, removes the dishcloth, and then—again first locating the woman's mouth by touch—uses her index finger to apply a thin coat of honey thinned with vodka to her lips.

The woman smacks her lips together. "Oh," she whispers. "Oh. Yes."

The insensible mechanics of the playground push together Jay and a boy named Charlie. Everyone agrees that Jay likes Charlie and Charlie likes Jay, and Jay is not unpleasantly swept along this current until it feels like it originated inside herself. Charlie is nice to her and has longish, floppy hair. At the end of the school day, as they're both walking across the blacktop with friends to the pickup area, she suddenly dashes across the divide and kisses him on the cheek.

Behind her, as she runs away toward her mother's car, mercifully already in the circular drive of the school, the kids holler and roar. She doesn't look back until she's in the car with the door safely shut. She spots Charlie, his hand lifted to his cheek as though he'd been wounded there, his mouth ajar.

Later that week, Charlie kisses her on the mouth under the stairs, a kiss long enough for Jay to close her eyes. The darkness behind her eyelids has a different quality in that moment than any she's ever known, defined by an occluding object—Charlie, the moon eclipsing the sun. Two months pass before they sit together on the bus on a field trip, the second row from the back. When his face dips to hers, she grabs on to his waist unthinkingly. Hard, her nails digging into his side. He jerks away and Jay opens her eyes. She still feels blurred, smudged like a streak of paint. She'd been reaching out toward that darkness.

Charlie looks terrified. And he looks to her, all at once, like the little boy he is. Like any of the other boys in their class, without his aura of specialness. And she understands the darkness is related to the kiss, to kissing, and not to Charlie himself.

Increasingly, Jay feels like the only time she spends with her mother is in the car on the drive to and from school. Allie takes it for granted that Jay will shower and brush her teeth and put herself to bed. She asks her if she's done her homework, but she no longer checks, no longer tries to help in her hapless way. (Jay was disturbed to find her class had already outstripped her mother's capabilities in mathematics.) Allie is always distracted by her new "projects." And she still eats, and she doesn't even bother to hide it. Earlier that week, she cooked a steak in butter—where did she even find such things anymore?—and filled the house with the most horrifying smell of rot and blood. She sat at the table gagging and grimacing, her jaw working and her cheeks bulging obscenely. Their last substantial interaction was a fight, over a year ago, when Allie found out Jay was throwing away the lunches she packed. "I'm the only kid who still brings food!" Jay screamed.

Allie picks up Jay after the field trip. The hatchback trunk is filled with multicolored rubber bouncy balls. Jay climbs into the front seat.

"How was the museum?"

"Good," Jay says. Her mother's attention is on the road, but Jay still turns her face away. She presses her hot cheek to the window. "Weird," she amends. She waits for Allie to ask her what was weird about it. She's certain Allie will notice the change in her. She feels like something fundamental and bodily happened on the bus, like her organs have liquefied inside her, to reform in new shapes in time. Charlie merely the vector, not the cause.

"Mmm," Allie says. "Do you have your house key? Do you mind if I just drop you off at home? I need to go to the hardware store."

"Can you be more specific?" Allie says.

"White. A good French bread, with a crisp crust," says the man on the phone.

"A baguette? Brioche?"

"No, like a rustic loaf. A boule. The kind you'd make at home in a Dutch oven. Do you know what I mean?"

"Oh yes. Butter? Oil and vinegar?"

"No, plain." He pauses. "When it's still hot and fresh from the oven. When you tap the crust to test it, and then saw through the first slice with a bread knife, and the inside, before it's touched the air, is almost like cake—" He laughs self-consciously. "It feels good just talking about it. I feel like I can almost taste it when I describe it to you. It's better than baking bread, certainly. I thought, even if I don't eat it, just going through the motions, measuring the ingredients, waiting for it to rise, kneading it . . . But it was awful somehow. Like making a puppet from a corpse."

"Have you been to the meetups?"

"I've heard about them. They sound so sad, just sitting around and talking about food. But now I'm not sure. Have you been?"

"No, I think it would distract from my . . ." Allie hesitates over what to call it. "From what I do," she says, finally. "But I get a lot of clients through them. They tell each other about me."

"I've heard you're a con artist."

"Really!"

"That you exploit . . . people like me."

"People like you?"

"You know. Desperate people. People who can't forget. There should be a word for us." He exhales heavily into the receiver. "I used to think everyone experienced food the way I did, a fundamental reason to live, right up there with sex. But now . . . I mean, imagine if everyone lost their ability to orgasm. God, maybe I should go to one of the meetups."

Allie is only half listening, still fixated on the idea of herself as a con artist. "Did you hear that from someone who actually came to see me?"

"No," he admits. "I heard it from my daughter."

"Your daughter?"

"She goes to school with yours."

Jay has always seemed so independent, so thoroughly un-interested in Allie's life or career, that Allie can't imagine *other children* talking about her.

"I heard you were a failed artist, before," he continues. "A conceptual artist, installations, performances. Under a different name."

"I was a web designer," she says. "With a degree in graphic design."

"But that's more or less what it is, right? Food-themed conceptual art?"

"I don't consider myself an artist." She realizes that isn't true. When she submerges a client in bouncy balls, when she carefully sets their leg hair on fire, when she contrives a thousand ways to make twitch this now-insensate limb, she feels like a poet, making concrete something that no longer has concrete manifestation in the world. Orange paint and silk for the soft-boiled egg that lives only in your heart. Smooth wood and sticky lips for the underripe pear that will never be again. She doesn't believe it's a con—but if it is, she doesn't care. It works, as well as any other placebo. "So when would you like to come?"

Soon afterward, Jay wakes to find she's huddled in a ball under the covers, and the tip of her nose is freezing above the comforter. "Mom," she calls. "What's wrong with the heat?"

"Nothing," Allie yells back. She's wearing two pairs of pants and two sweaters layered. "I turned it off last night. Get ready for school. It'll be warm there."

After she's dropped off Jay and returned home, Allie empties their shared bathroom of towels and any visible knick-knacks and body products. She's surprised at the number of half-finished tubes and bottles that she doesn't recognize, more surprised to find a cheap pink razor that isn't her own. She files this away for a later conversation with Jay.

She runs the shower at its hottest, filling the bathroom with steam as the porcelain floor tiles remain paradoxically cold. She covers the cleared vanity and shelves and the closed toilet lid and tank with wood wick candles, advertised to crackle continuously. She dusts their wicks in calcium chloride, and when she lights them, the flames are a hyperreal orange, like fire in an old video game, or through the filter of memory. The sound is as warm and irregular as dust on a vinyl record.

When her client arrives, the classic French boule, she has him sit on the cold bathroom floor, surrounded by strangely colored candlelight and steam, the crackle of crust. She wraps him in a weighted blanket. She slips a baseball-sized wad of cheap modeling clay into his hands, fresh from the packet, still hard. Wordlessly, she gestures for him to work the clay in his hands. She closes the door and leaves him alone.

He emerges about twenty minutes later. His eyes are red and filmy. "Thank you," he says. She nods. He leaves hurriedly. He's a tall man, and he looks awkward and oversized putting on his winter clothes in their small foyer with its child-height hooks, the ones Jay is already outgrowing. He forgets his gloves on the bench. Allie sees Jay studying the large, unfamiliar gloves as she takes off her own coat and boots that afternoon, but Jay doesn't ask, so Allie doesn't explain.

At the end of P.E. class, Jay's teacher calls her over and asks her if she'd be willing to join the track team. They're short kids for several of the events, and Jay is obviously the fastest runner in her grade.

Six weeks later, Jay wins the eight-hundred-meter dash at the district meet, one of the last events of the day. As she nears the finish line, her focus winnows, the smattering of people in the stands and the other girls close at her heels and the red clay track beneath her—all of it blurs and distorts. Her feet lighten, she feels airborne, soaring and surging, every resource within her rallied.

She stands on the podium, still breathless, and a painted plastic medal is hung around her neck. Her teammates are screaming, both her name and guttural shrieks of glee. Jay wants to cry, she wants to throw herself into someone's arms, she wants to take off running again. The steely winter sky, streaked with color as the afternoon ends, is unspeakably beautiful.

As the meet took place during a school day, Allie is one of the few parents who could come to watch. She hugs Jay with one arm as they walk to the parking lot together. "I'm so proud of you," she says. "You're always so good at everything."

Jay doesn't know why, but this second sentence rankles her. She doesn't answer for a long moment, and when she does, she says, "Did you do sports when you were in school, Mom?"

"Me? Oh, no. I wasn't very athletic. Not like you."

In the car, Jay puts her headphones on. She cues up her favorite song of the moment, a female rapper with a dragging voice. The song calls up scraps of feeling—the darkness of Charlie's kiss, the high of the race—only in a lower key, near yet far, producing a sting of longing in her chest. Her mother doesn't chastise her for retreating into her headphones in the middle of a conversation the way a lot of her friends' parents do. She wants to ask her mother what bands she liked when she was a kid, who was the first boy she kissed, the first time she tasted victory and wanted it to last forever. She can't imagine her mother at her own age. Deep down, she doesn't believe Allie ever felt this way, this open and raw, flooded with wonder.

Jay lies in the window nook of Allie's office playing on her phone, her feet on the frame, her lanky body in leggings and a sweatshirt contorting into hieroglyphic shapes. Allie is altering her miniature plant bower with spiky holly boughs, which will hang near but not touch the skin of the client who asked for Chinese greens sautéed with garlic.

"What does this guy look like?" Jay asks.

"What guy?"

"The one you're building that thing for."

"I don't know. We've only emailed."

"Can I try it?"

"Try what?"

"Can I go inside?"

"Oh." Allie rocks the structure gently. It seems stable. "Sure, I guess so."

Jay jumps down from the window seat. She lies on her stomach on the floor and military-crawls through the entrance. "Be careful," Allie says. "The holly leaves are sharp."

"Now what?" Jay says from inside, her voice muffled.

Allie moves her color-filtered box light so, from the inside, it shines through the leaves like an alien sun, a watery olive tone behind the darker green of the holly. When Jay doesn't say anything, Allie says, "It's a work in progress."

After a moment, Jay reverse-crawls back out. "It does look cool in there." Her tone is magnanimous, like Allie is the child to be humored.

"You don't get it," Allie says. "You're too young."

Jay shrugs. She glides on the wood floor in her socks toward the door. She glances back at her mother over her narrow shoulders, her expression knowing, almost haughty, suggesting she's privy to any number of things that Allie doesn't understand. And Allie realizes Jay will never understand. The people demanding Allie's services will be gone in a generation. She doesn't create sensations, she awakens the memory of them, and only in those who are primed for it, who want badly to return to those memories, who want to believe. There are internet rumors about unaffected, isolated communities in the Amazon, but Allie knows these will turn out apocryphal in the end. The sensuous, life-affirming pleasure upon which whole cultures were built, which caused empires to rise and fall, will die with Allie and her peers.

Allie walks to the window where Jay had been sitting. Jay has gone outside without a jacket or hat. A thin, hard layer of snow covers their front lawn. Her headphones in, Jay is dancing, tossing her head, pirouetting on a booted foot. The snow sparkles around her, the winter sun low and blinding. Jay wraps her arms around her middle, still swaying, the picture of joy.

ACKNOWLEDGMENTS

"Liddy, First to Fly" was commissioned for publication in *Room* magazine 41.1 (2018).

"Time Cubes" was commissioned for performance at the Hugo House Literary Series (2018).

"In This Fantasy" was published in the 2018 *Short Story Advent Calendar* (Hingston & Olsen, 2018).

"Scissors" was published in *Kink*, edited by R.O. Kwon and Garth Greenwell (Simon & Schuster, 2021).

To Masie Cochran, exactly the right editor for this book in every way, for her boundless insight, enthusiasm, vision, and care.

To Craig Popelars, Becky Kraemer, Nanci McCloskey, Jakob Vala, Sangi Lama, Alyssa Ogi, Elizabeth DeMeo, Alex Gonzales, and everyone at Tin House, a team of consummate pros. To copyeditor Anne Horowitz and proofreader Shasta Clinch. To designer Jaya Miceli and art director Diane Chonette for the perfect cover. To my agent Jackie Kaiser, and to Meg Wheeler, Bridgette Kam, and everyone at Westwood Creative Artists. To Crystal Sikma, James Lindsay, Alana Wilcox, and everyone at Coach House Books.

To Garth Greenwell, R.O. Kwon, Alissa McArthur, Michael Hingston, Rob Arnold, Peter Mountford, Christopher DiRaddo, and Alma García, for inspiring these stories or giving them homes.

To Danya Kukafka, Danielle Mohlman, and Lucy Tan, brilliant writers and supportive friends, who light up every week and make this tenuous, unreal life I've chosen feel real. To Katrina Carrasco, Randi Eicher, and Sonora Jha, for holding space and writing alongside me in coffeeshops, libraries, and Zoom purgatory as these stories came together. To Catherine Case, whose friendship reminds me that creative joy is bigger than any one work or art form. To Tim Mak, who knows where the bodies are buried.

To my loving family: the Fus, the Fu-Loys, the Fu-Negilskis, the Loboses, and the Lobos-Dutrizacs.

To andrea bennett, my ideal reader and dearest friend, who kept this book alive in its earliest forms and darkest days. Who has kept me alive in my earliest forms and darkest days.

To JP, for a love beyond words.